THE BLACKGAARD CHRONICLES™

BOOK THREE

CROSS-CHECK

THE BLACKGAARD CHRONICLES™

BOOK THREE

CROSS-CHECK

PHIL LOLLAR

Tyndale House Publishers, Inc.
Carol Stream, Illinois

The Blackgaard Chronicles: *Cross-Check*
© 2019 Focus on the Family. All rights reserved.

Illustrations © 2019 Focus on the Family

A Focus on the Family book published by Tyndale House Publishers, Inc., Carol Stream, Illinois 60188

Adventures in Odyssey, Focus on the Family, and their accompanying logos and designs are federally registered trademarks of Focus on the Family, 8605 Explorer Drive, Colorado Springs, CO 80920. The Blackgaard Chronicles is a trademark of Focus on the Family.

TYNDALE and Tyndale's quill logo are registered trademarks of Tyndale House Publishers, Inc.

This book is based on Adventures in Odyssey audio drama episodes "The Nemesis, Part 1" and "The Nemesis, Part 2"—original scripts by Phil Lollar.

Novelization by Phil Lollar

Editor: Larry Weeden

Cover design by Jacob Isom

Cover illustration by Gary Locke

For Library of Congress Cataloging-in-Publication data for this title, visit: http://www.loc.gov/help/contract-general.html.

For manufacturing information regarding this product, please call 1-800-323-9400.

For information about special discounts for bulk purchases, please contact Tyndale House Publishers at csresponse@tyndale.com, or call 1-800-323-9400.

ISBN 978-1-58997-981-9

Printed in China

25	24	23	22	21	20	19
7	6	5	4	3	2	1

For

Hal Smith

and

Walker Edmiston

Don't miss *Opening Moves* and *Pawn's Play*, books 1 and 2 in The Blackgaard Chronicles book series. Available from better bookstores everywhere and at www.WhitsEnd.org/Store.

The Blackgaard Chronicles are based on the popular Adventures in Odyssey (AIO) audio drama series. Learn more at www.aioclub.org, including how to get access to the complete library of AIO episodes, exclusive AIO radio dramas, daily devotions, and much more.

CHAPTER ONE

Dr. Regis Blackgaard exploded with fury. "Expelled, Richard?" he shouted. "You got expelled from Campbell College over a lousy grade-changing scheme!"

The speakerphone on Philip Glossman's desk distorted with the volume of the outburst. Richard Maxwell winced at the sound and stared across the desk at Glossman, who leaned back in his office chair, arms crossed over his potbelly, smiling blissfully at the verbal lashing Maxwell was receiving.

"I thought you were smart—even clever! But apparently you don't even have any common sense! Why would you do something so idiotic?"

Maxwell shrugged. "Hey, you cut off my extra income from the retirement home, remember?"

"You've jeopardized this operation for a little 'extra income'?"

"I didn't jeopardize—"

"You could have been arrested! You could have attracted police attention—"

"But I wasn't and I didn't, thanks to Whittaker. I knew he'd convince them to not get the police involved." Maxwell smirked. "He's a goody-two-shoes like the rest of them—the biggest one of all, in fact. He's all about giving people second chances."

Blackgaard's voice turned deadly. "Well, I am *not* about giving people second chances, Richard."

Maxwell suppressed the chill that went down his spine. He opened his mouth to respond when Glossman leaned forward and cut in. "Of course, the worst part in all of this is that you didn't get Applesauce," Glossman said. "You didn't even *try*. And now, you won't be able to." He leaned back and smiled once again.

You're just loving this, aren't you, councilman? Maxwell thought. *Well, see how much you love this. . . .* He sniffed and said aloud, "Actually, I did try."

Glossman's smile evaporated. The speakerphone sat silent. Maxwell tapped on it and said, "Hello? Did we lose you there, Doc?"

"You tried to download Applesauce?"

"Yep."

"And? What happened?"

Maxwell shrugged again. "I couldn't do it from that computer."

Glossman leaned forward and put his hands on the desk. "Wait a minute," he said. "Back at the warehouse, you said you *could* do it on that computer!"

"*Maybe*," Maxwell retorted. "I said *maybe* I could do it. Turns out Burglemeister may be a coot, but he's no dope. He knows his stuff. He wrote in a subroutine that notifies him when the system is being used for purposes other than those for which it was designed.

I had to cover my tracks, so I hid what I did under what Meltsner was doing. That's how Burglemeister nailed him for changing the grades back."

"But you still got caught," Glossman sneered.

"Yeah, well, I thought I had better control over little Nicky," Maxwell replied. "Who knew? The point is I couldn't have used that computer. I'm gonna need a dedicated computer with its own access and a secure, private place to operate it from." He stared at Glossman. "Assuming, that is, that we'll actually *get* such a place. How's the Gower's Landing shopping complex acquisition coming, Glossy? Mansfield Computers still givin' you fits?"

Glossman's face reddened and contorted with rage. He popped out of his chair and started for Maxwell. "You slimy little sneak!" he roared. "I oughta—"

"Sit down, Philip!" Blackgaard commanded.

Glossman stopped and gaped at the speakerphone, then slowly sank back into his chair.

Maxwell was impressed. How did Blackgaard know Glossman had jumped up? Did he have a video camera in this office? Maxwell restrained himself from glancing around the room as Blackgaard continued.

"He's right," Blackgaard said. "We still don't have the building secured. And now, apparently, we're going to need it more than ever."

Glossman tugged at his collar. "I'm meeting with Webster again tomorrow, sir," he said nervously. "We'll do everything we can."

Maxwell chuckled and said, "So far that hasn't been much." Glossman started to rise again, but Maxwell put up his hands. "Sorry—cheap shot. Listen, boys, I think I can help you out here."

Glossman scowled. "You think—"

"Quiet, Philip," Blackgaard ordered. "Do go on, Richard."

Maxwell grinned and winked at Glossman, whose face reddened again. Maxwell rose from his chair and paced the room. "Before I came here today, I stopped by Odyssey Retirement Home."

"Stealing from them again?" sneered Glossman.

Maxwell chuckled. "Oh, no, no. Nothing like that.

y hi to some of the old folks there—

named Mary Hooper. Sad case, really.

t her in the home when her husband died. ed putting her in several homes, actually, but she got kicked out of them all, so they ended up at ORH. Easy to see why: She's not a very nice person. She's grouchy, snippy, and downright mean most of the time—even to kids like my sister's friend Donna. I wouldn't want her living with me, either. She sort of made up with her daughter a few weeks back, but I can tell you firsthand that Mary Hooper does not like her son-in-law. *At. All.*"

"I'm getting bored, Richard," Blackgaard said.

Maxwell slid back into his chair. "While I was at the home, I checked the records, Doc. Found out two very interesting things. Y'know, they really need to improve their security. I mean, it *is* private information, after all—"

"The *point*, Richard!"

Maxwell smiled. He knew he shouldn't do it, but he loved testing Blackgaard's patience. It was so easy.

"First, ORH has quite a few code violations—*city* code violations."

Glossman sat up.

Maxwell's smile broadened, and he leaned in toward the speakerphone. "And second: Mary Hooper's son-in-law . . . is Bob Mansfield . . . owner of Mansfield Computers."

There was a pause. Glossman's eyes darted alternately between the phone and Maxwell. When a deep chuckle wafted through the speaker, the councilman smirked unctuously in spite of himself.

"Very good, Richard," Blackgaard intoned. "A recovery from your blunder at the college."

Maxwell thought about sneering at the phone, but then he remembered the hidden camera and instead just nodded graciously and smiled.

Blackgaard went on: "You know what to do with this information, Philip?"

"I can think of one or two things, yes," Glossman replied, still smirking.

"Richard, get Philip the specifics on what you will

need computer-wise. If this is handled properly, we can kill two birds with one stone."

Maxwell couldn't help twisting the knife. "That's a big *if*," he said. "Need any help with that, Glossy?"

Glossman's smirk faded. "I'll handle it on my own, thanks."

Blackgaard's voice turned dark. "Make sure you do, Philip."

CHAPTER TWO

Sometimes after a problem has stymied you for a long time, when a solution presents itself, the speed with which the problem is solved can be mind-boggling. Glossman marveled at the rapidity with which the takeover of the Mansfield Computers property happened during the next few days. All it took was a phone call, and a whirlwind of nefarious activity spun up in Odyssey, though almost none of the participants knew its roots—at least not completely—nor that the whirlwind was aimed squarely at Bob Mansfield.

Glossman's call was to a colleague of his, a city inspector named Noah Ewell—who just happened to be the brother-in-law of Holden Webster of Webster Development. Ewell then paid a surprise visit to the Odyssey Retirement Home.

After a haphazard examination of the facility and a cursory perusal of its records, Ewell instantly proclaimed the home in violation of several ordinances and codes. He ordered Molly Helprin, ORH's director, to bring the facility up to city standards immediately or it would have to be shut down.

When Helprin asked if there were any way to avoid that, Ewell said she could delay the shutdown by first calling the family of a specific ORH resident—one Mary Hooper.

Helprin called Hooper's daughter, Barbara Mansfield, and informed her of the pending shutdown, and that Barbara would have to come and get Mary. Upon completing that conversation, Barbara naturally and immediately called her husband, Bob, at his computer store.

The whirlwind had turned into a tornado and had plopped down right in Bob Mansfield's office.

He hung up the phone on his desk and sighed heavily. This couldn't be happening. Not again. His mother-in-law was getting kicked out of yet *another* facility—which meant she would have to move in with them.

He remembered the last time that happened. It was nonstop fighting. His mother-in-law never missed an opportunity to put him down, going so far as dredging up hot-button issues from ten years ago. And, he had to admit, he often gave as good as he got, though he tried not to.

In the end, it was simply too much. They had decided that for the stability of their own home, they needed to put her in a facility. But she proved just as mean and hateful in all of them, and one by one, they refused to keep her.

Barbara and he finally found Odyssey Retirement

Home, which assured them that the only way it would turn her away was if it closed down, a situation they were further assured was next to impossible. And now, the impossible was apparently very possible.

Mansfield removed his horned-rimmed glasses, set them on his desk, and leaned his lanky frame back in his office chair, which squeaked faintly at the move. He squinched his eyes, pinched the bridge of his thin nose where his glasses normally sat, moved his bony hand up through his thick, brown hair and down his neck, giving his nape a brief massage. He couldn't bear having Mary back in his home again, he just couldn't!

Even though Mary and Barbara had supposedly made up recently—Barbara said they'd actually had a warm and wonderful moment together—he was skeptical it would last long. Especially if they were forced to live in the same house. Mary was just too set in her ways. And she'd never liked him. No, it just wouldn't do.

His thoughts were interrupted by a knock on his office door. He sat up and called out, "Come in." The door opened to reveal someone he didn't want to see almost as much as he didn't want to see his mother-in-law. Mansfield exhaled heavily, dropped his chin to his chest, and growled, "What do you want, Webster?"

Holden Webster oozed his squat, oily, rotund form into the room. His fleshy face was all smiles. "I was just in the neighborhood and thought I'd pop in and see if you'd changed your mind about my offer," he said.

"I really don't need this today, Webster," Mansfield replied.

Webster moved toward the desk, still smiling. "Oh, c'mon now! I bet you need it more than you realize!"

Mansfield looked at him incredulously. "Are you thick or something? For the last time, no! I'm not interested in moving!"

Webster's face turned solemn. "Are you sure? It really is a sweet deal. Buying out your lease, moving you to a new location—all expenses paid. You really have nothing to lose."

"I've already lost something," Mansfield snapped. "My patience!"

Webster chuckled loudly. "Good one! But seriously—this deal won't last forever."

"Is that a promise?"

Webster raised his chubby hands. "I mean it! Once it's off the table, it's O-F-F off!"

Mansfield mimicked his movements. "Then let it be O-F-F off, and you O-U-T out!" He jabbed his finger toward the door, then turned his attention to a stack of papers on his desk.

Webster lowered his hands, smiled shrewdly, and shook his head slightly, jiggling his multiple chins. "Okay. Have it your way." He walked back to the door, put his hand on the knob, and then said, "Oh, one more thing: How's your mother-in-law?"

Mansfield stopped shuffling papers, looked up, and blinked. "What?"

Webster still faced the door. "I think you heard me."

"What do you know about my mother-in-law?"

Webster turned around, a look of mock concern on his face. "Just that she may need new living arrangements very soon."

A chill went down Mansfield's spine. "How did you . . ."

Webster walked back and sank his bulk into a chair in front of the desk. "My brother-in-law is a code inspector for the city. He might've mentioned it, y'know, in passing."

Mansfield's mind was starting to spin. "Your brother-in-law mentioned *my* mother-in-law to you?"

"Well, not her specifically, but he did say that because of code violations, all those poor folks at the home would have to find new living arrangements." Webster shook his head, jiggling his chins again. "Sad."

"How . . . how did you even know my mother-in-law lived there? Have you been spying on me or something?"

Webster winced. "*Spying* is such a creepy word . . . I prefer *researching.*"

Mansfield felt his face getting hot, and he clenched his fists. "Research about what? What's going on here? Why is what happens to my mother-in-law any of your business?"

"Because I'm your friend," Webster said sincerely. "And I want to help you."

"Friend?" Mansfield scoffed. "Since when? And help me how?"

The portly man leaned forward, the chair moaning under his girth, and rested his beefy forearm on the desk. "Suppose I told you that it's possible for your mother-in-law to stay where she is?" he said evenly. "Would that be worth something to you?"

"Worth something? What do you mean?"

Webster smirked. "Now who's being thick?"

Mansfield's eyes narrowed. "This building? You want me to trade my mother-in-law's living arrangements . . . for this building?"

Webster just smiled.

Mansfield's jaw hardened. "Get out of my office," he said through gritted teeth.

"Now, now, no need for hostility—"

Mansfield bolted out of his chair and slammed his hands on his desk. "You're trying to extort me!"

"Not extort, *help*—"

"Get out of my office before I throw you out!"

Webster hoisted himself up from the chair. "Okay, okay, take it easy!" He made his way to the door, opened it, and stepped through. "When you're ready, you know how to get in touch with me."

"Out!"

The door closed. Mansfield shook with fury. The gall! The unmitigated gall! That blackmailer would not take his building from him! If that meant his mother-in-law had to move in with him again—as unpleasant a prospect as that was—then so be it! Maybe her reconciliation with Barbara would make things different this time.

He picked up the phone and called his wife. "Barbara? It's Bob. Get a room ready. We're bringing your mother home."

But even the stiffest of resolve can crumble in the face of reality. The following day, Bob, Barbara, and their two kids went to pick up Mary Hooper from Odyssey Retirement Home. Within ten minutes of their arrival, Mary had insulted Bob three times, screamed at

Barbara, and made both of her grandchildren run from the room crying.

After comforting his family, Bob went to the phone in the lobby and dialed Webster's number. The oily voice answered, "Webster Development."

"You win," Mansfield said.

"I'm sorry, who is this?" Webster replied.

"You know who it is—Bob Mansfield!"

"Bob!" Webster said cheerily. "How can I help you?"

Mansfield fumed. "You wanna play games? Fine. Upon reflection, I've concluded that forcing all these senior citizens out of their home just so I can keep my building would be . . . wrong. So tell your brother-in-law to call it off. You can have the building. I'll take your deal."

"Well, that's fine, Bob!" Webster's voice gushed from the receiver. "We'll be happy to take the building. But what do you mean by 'deal'?"

"You know what I mean! You buy out my lease and pay to move me to a new location!"

"Oh, yes!" Webster responded. "I'm sorry, but that

deal is off the table, remember? I'm afraid you'll have to do all that on your own."

"Are you insane?" Mansfield hissed into the phone. "Do you know how much money that'll cost me?"

"As a matter of fact, I do."

"If you think I'm going to hand over my building without getting something for it, you're—"

Just then, he heard Mary scream at his wife once again from down the hall, and a second later, he saw Barbara burst from the room in tears. Webster's voice grated in his ear from the phone. "Hello, Bob? Are you there?"

Mansfield sighed heavily. "Fine," he said. "I'll pay for everything. I'll be out by the end of the week."

"Wonderful!" Webster chimed. "Oh, there's just one more thing."

"What now?"

Mansfield heard Webster shuffle papers around. "Ah, here it is. When you move, I'm going to need you to leave behind some special computer equipment . . ."

CHAPTER THREE

Mansfield was true to his word. He was completely moved out of the building by the end of the week. Webster Development then quickly finalized the purchase of the whole Gower's Landing shopping complex. Two days later, a large set of keys were sent, special delivery, from Webster to a seemingly abandoned warehouse in Chicago.

The following evening, a tall, lean, angular-featured man with a jet-black mustache and Vandyke, dressed in a perfectly tailored black three-piece suit, walked up to the front doors of the empty Gower's Landing. He carried a black walking stick with a polished gold knob for a handle in one hand and cradled a large, fluffy, gray Persian cat in the crook of his other arm. He shifted the walking stick to his other hand, pulled the keys from his coat pocket, selected one from the mass on the ring, unlocked the doors, and slipped inside, locking them after him.

Dr. Regis Blackgaard surveyed the empty, cavernous space in front of him, smiled, and nodded approvingly. Gower's Landing was finally his.

"It'll have to be gutted, of course—rebuilt almost from the ground up," he said with a scowl to the cat. "And we'll have to do something about that name, Sasha. The new one will have to be something attractive to kids. Something like . . . Palace?"

Sasha meowed.

"No, no, you're right—too feminine."

He noticed the building was not quite empty after all. A stack of boxes sat in the middle of the space. He crossed to them, his footsteps echoing off the walls, and examined the labels. Computer equipment left behind by Mansfield. These would make that twerp Maxwell happy.

"Now, now, be generous," he muttered to himself. Sasha purred. Richard was annoying, but he had proved to be quite useful and would no doubt continue to. Still, he bore careful watching; the lad was smart—too smart for his own good, smart enough to discover the real purpose behind the acquisition of Gower's Landing.

Blackgaard reached into his breast coat pocket and withdrew two large sheets of paper that had been folded several times. He unfolded them to reveal that the top sheet was the blueprints of the building. He consulted them briefly, folded the papers under his arm, and crossed the room to a door marked "Private."

He selected another key from the massive ring, unlocked the door, opened it, and found himself at the top of a long staircase. He placed the keys back in his pocket and retrieved from it a small flashlight, which he clicked on and then descended into the darkness.

"Fortress! A fine, strong name, and the place certainly reminds me of one!"

Sasha meowed again.

"Yes, good point—too masculine, and perhaps a bit too on-the-nose for my purposes."

At the bottom of the stairs, he shone the light ahead of him. It illumined a long hallway. The ceiling was lined with piping. The floor was covered with dust and spare piping. Two small rats glared at him, their beady eyes twinkling in the flashlight beam. Sasha hissed at them, and they scurried off to safety. Apparently neither Mansfield nor the other former business owners at Gower's Landing came down here much. *Good.*

Blackgaard made his way slowly down the hall. On his left was a series of doors marked "Electric," "Janitorial," and "Storage." He shone the flashlight beam to the end of the hallway and could barely make out another door marked "Office," though it looked as if it hadn't been used for that purpose for quite some time.

None of these interested him. His concern was with the wall on his right. It had no doors—at least, none that were visible.

He inched along, using the knob of his cane to rap on the bare wall as he went . . . *tap, tap, tap* . . . it had to be here somewhere . . . *tap, tap, tap* . . . c'mon now . . . *tap, tap, tap* . . . it should be riiiight—*tap, tap, thunk!*— here. *Thunk!* Yes!

He lowered Sasha to the floor, leaned his cane against the janitorial door, stuffed the papers into his side coat pocket, and propped the flashlight next to the cane so it illuminated the wall. Then he retrieved one of the pieces of piping from the musty floor and gave the wall a hard whack right at the *thunk!* point.

Sasha recoiled. The pipe went through the plaster, crumbling it.

"Sorry, Sasha," Blackgaard said, but he hit the spot again and again and again, and each blow brought down more of the wall. Soon he had uncovered its treasure: a door.

Winded, he dropped the pipe, picked up the flashlight and cane, selected a very old key from the ring, unlocked the secret door, and pushed it open. Sasha preceded him into the dark space.

Inside, the flashlight revealed a large room built of very old bricks on a stone foundation with a paneled Victorian-era patinated tin ceiling. It was empty and surprisingly clean, though the floor was dusty, and cobwebs strung its corners. Yes, once sterilized and the electricity was turned on, the room would do nicely—the perfect space for a private laboratory.

But there was more to the room than just space. It contained the real reason he wanted—*needed*—this building. He shone the flashlight around the walls and saw it. Opposite from the door into the room was another door—old, metal, bolted shut in three places. He bounded across the room to it, jimmied the rusted bolts free, and pulled it open.

Behind it, a tunnel stretched into the darkness.

Blackgaard chuckled with delight, retrieved the papers from his pocket, unfolded them, and this time consulted the second one. It was very old, so old that he'd had it encased in plastic. Printed across the top in ornate lettering were the words "Odyssey Passageways." Below them was a map of what at first glance appeared to be roads around town, but upon closer inspection was actually a network of interwoven tunnels connecting various spots in town with various other spots.

He aimed the beam from his flashlight at one of the spots. It read "Gower's Landing." There was a drawing of what appeared to be a barn there, no doubt the property of the original owner before it was torn down to build a shopping center. A passageway—the very one that yawned before him—led away from the barn.

Blackgaard followed the path with the light. It curved through the field, intersected with other tunnels, made several twists and turns, and finally, all the way across town, connected to the middle of what looked like a bigger tunnel, forming a T. Turn left at the T and the tunnel meandered out to some woods. Turn right and the tunnel led almost directly to the drawing of an old Victorian mansion. Below it was printed "Odyssey Church." He had drawn a line through that and had written under it "Fillmore Recreation Center"; then a line through that, and under it written "Whit's End."

How old Professor M. had gotten this map was a mystery, the solution to which he never divulged. It didn't matter anyhow; he had the map now, and it would be put to great use, not only as a means to Whittaker's place, but also as a way to move equipment discreetly into his new business.

Assuming, that is, that Glossman would be able to secure the Odyssey town council's approval of the license to operate this new business. The incompetent weasel had assured him it was in the bag, but he'd done that before. No matter; he, Blackgaard, had leaned on Glossman before and would do it again if necessary.

Blackgaard looked back into the cavernous underground room, and the thought crossed his mind of how perfect a dungeon it would make, just like in the castles of old. "Wait!" he said aloud. "That's it! That's what

I'll call this place—the difference between a palace and a fortress: a castle!"

He felt Sasha rub against his leg, and he shone the flashlight down on her. She gazed up at him quizzically.

He frowned again. "You're right . . . we can't just call it 'The Castle.'" It needs a more descriptive name, more definitive. But should he? Dare he? Did he really want to be that visible a presence around town? He looked back into the tunnel. "Well, why not?" he said softly. Now that he'd found this access, the business above would be the perfect cover for his doings down here. He smiled broadly and said aloud the name he was visualizing on his new business license:

"Blackgaard's Castle."

He shone the light down on his cat once again. "What do you think, Sasha?"

She purred and rubbed up against his legs affection-ately.

Perfect.

CHAPTER FOUR

I t was happening *again*.

Dr. Regis Blackgaard surveyed the Odyssey Town Council from behind the lectern facing them at the council chamber. Though outwardly calm, inwardly he was seething. Why did he keep relying on that complete nincompoop Philip Glossman to get things done?

Glossman had failed to get him the Fillmore Recreation building five years ago. He had failed to secure the Gower's Landing complex last month. And now he was failing to get approval for the business license for Blackgaard's Castle.

Glossman had been adamant that getting approval for the license would be a mere formality. Yet he had been arguing the point for the past 45 minutes with Tom Riley, the yokel farmer who was also on the council and who apparently had far more sway on it than did Glossman. The two of them hammered away at each other from their executive chairs behind the large conference table at the front of the room. Glossman was sweating even more than usual, and as his voice rose, his face grew redder and redder.

"We're clouding the issue!" Glossman shouted. "The motion before this council is whether to grant a business license to Dr. Regis Blackgaard." Glossman gestured toward him. "Why all this discussion about the *type* of business?"

Riley leaned forward in his chair. "Because we don't want just *any* business moving into town, Mr. Glossman," he said.

"But we know what type of business it is, Councilman Riley—an amusement house for kids."

"An amusement house." Riley frowned and turned his gaze to Blackgaard. "No offense, Mr. Blackgaard, but that sounds pretty vague to me. Would you mind explaining just what an 'amusement house' *is*?"

Blackgaard smiled benignly and replied charmingly, "A house that amuses people, of course. In this case, children."

Riley nodded. "Mmm. Well, just what kinds of amusements are we talking about?"

"Oh, any number of things: electronic devices . . . games . . . displays—"

Glossman jumped in. "Will you serve food?"

Blackgaard fought the impulse to snap at him for the interruption. "Yes. Nothing big, just snacks and things of that nature."

Riley's brow furrowed. "What nature?"

Glossman fell back in his chair, exasperated. "Oh, Mr. Riley! Why must you be so specific? Blackgaard's Castle sounds very similar to Whit's End to me."

It was Riley's turn to smile benignly. "Well, now, that's another thing that surprises me, Mr. Glossman. As I recollect, you were against this type of place when Mr. Whittaker opened Whit's End. Why the change of mind?"

Tactical error, Philip, thought Blackgaard. *Yet another blunder.*

"I didn't change my mind, Councilman Riley," Glossman sneered. "I wasn't against Mr. Whittaker opening his establishment. I merely felt the land could be put to better use. Now that I've seen how successful such a place can be, I think we should have more of them. It'll promote competition, which can only help the local economy."

"*If* Blackgaard's Castle is like Whit's End, Mr. Glossman," Riley replied. "That's what we still have to determine."

Glossman huffed. "Look, we know as much about Blackgaard's Castle as we knew about Whit's End before it opened."

Riley shook his head. "'Fraid I'm gonna have to

differ with you there, Mr. Glossman. We knew quite
a bit more about Mr. Whittaker's plans than we do
about Mr. Blackgaard's." He gestured to a spot in the
gallery behind Blackgaard. "In fact, I'd like to ask Mr.
Whittaker if he'd come up and read the goals he had in
mind before he started Whit's End. Mr. Whittaker?"

Blackgaard turned, and for an instant he was genuinely surprised. Apparently he'd been so irritated with
Glossman's poor performance that he'd failed to notice
the owner of Whit's End entering the chamber. As
quickly as the surprise struck him, Blackgaard suppressed it. He relinquished the lectern with a polite
nod as Whittaker approached.

Whittaker returned the nod and smiled pleasantly
as he stepped onto the rostrum and took from his coat
pocket a worn piece of paper.

"Thank you, Councilman Riley, but many of these
were *my wife's* last wishes," Whittaker began. He carefully unfolded the paper and read the feminine hand-
writing on it. "Whit's End is designed to be a place
of adventure and discovery, filled with books and

activities, arts and crafts, and uplifting conversation. But most of all, it is a place where kids—of all ages—can just be kids."

He refolded the paper, put it back in his coat pocket, nodded at Riley, and stepped away from the lectern and off the rostrum.

"Thank you, Mr. Whittaker," Riley said, and then he turned to Blackgaard. "Can you promise this council that your business will be all those things, Mr. Blackgaard?"

Blackgaard stepped back behind the lectern, and for the second time that morning he allowed a genuine feeling to break his facade of calm—not surprise this time, but irritation. The curt words escaped his lips before he could stop them: "Excuse me, Councilman Riley, but my title is *Doctor* Regis Blackgaard. I worked very hard to attain it, and I'd appreciate it if you'd remember it."

Riley sat back and blinked. "Oh! I'm sorry, Doctor."

An unctuous smile curled Glossman's lips as he said, "That's something that should've been mentioned earlier. Dr. Blackgaard has a PhD, with an emphasis in child psychology. I think that more than qualifies him to open up an amusement house for children, don't you?"

Riley's gaze hardened. "Maybe, maybe not," he said. "It still depends on what kind of place he wants to open up!"

Both men glared at each other for a moment, and then both lurched forward in their chairs.

"Now, look, Riley—!"

"Mr. Glossman, you need to—!"

"Excuse me!" Whittaker shouted. "Excuse me!" He remounted the rostrum and leaned in to the lectern microphone to say, "Uh, excuse me, gentlemen, but if I may, I'd like to make a suggestion."

Riley ringed out an ear with his index finger. "What is it, Mr. Whittaker?" he asked.

"This issue has come up very fast, so perhaps Dr. Blackgaard hasn't had time to outline what he'd like to do with Blackgaard's Castle. Would it be possible to delay the vote for a week so he can provide more details about his new business? Then the council can decide."

Glossman looked ready to explode.

This has gone on long enough, thought Blackgaard, and he leaned in to the mic. "I think that's an excellent suggestion, Mr. Whittaker," he said.

Glossman immediately sat back in his chair, the color draining from his face.

Riley also eased back and looked at him. "Councilman Glossman?" Riley asked.

Glossman wiped the sweat from his brow, fixed his gaze on Blackgaard, and said curtly, "If everyone agrees, who am I to stand in the way?"

Blackgaard raised an eyebrow, and Glossman quickly looked away.

Riley reached for his gavel. "Good," he said. "Let the minutes show that the vote to grant a business license to Dr. Regis Blackgaard to open the establishment called Blackgaard's Castle was postponed until one week from today. This meeting is adjourned."

He pounded the gavel, and the meeting broke up with the usual buzz and low conversations that accompany such events. Blackgaard turned to the man next to him on the rostrum and said, "Thank you, Mr. Whittaker."

"Well, you looked like you could use some help, Dr. Blackgaard," Whittaker responded, smiling. "I know how difficult it can be to appear before a town council—especially this one."

Blackgaard forced a congenial chuckle. "Mr. Glossman and Mr. Riley certainly don't see eye to eye. I must say that I didn't anticipate this much trouble in simply getting a business license, though."

Whittaker nodded. "The people of Odyssey are good folks, Dr. Blackgaard. They get involved in their community."

"Yes, I'm beginning to see that."

Riley and Glossman approached them, still engaged in verbal battle. Whittaker jumped in again. "Hey, you two, don't make me intervene again!" he said. "The meeting's over."

Glossman and Riley both stopped, and the latter chuckled. "Just cleanin' up some loose ends," Riley said. "Dr. Blackgaard, I hope there's no hard feelings about what went on today. Mr. Glossman'll tell you that people around here are very particular about the kinds of business they want in town."

"Yes," Glossman growled, "but you can carry being 'particular' too far."

This time Blackgaard jumped in before they could start up again. "Gentlemen, gentlemen," he said, "Mr. Whittaker is correct. The meeting is over for today. No, Mr. Riley, there are no hard feelings. I know you're just doing your job. I'm sure this matter will be cleared up next week."

Riley nodded and smiled warmly. "Well, I hope so, Dr. Blackgaard."

"Mr. Riley and I are going over to my place to get something to drink," Whittaker added. "Would you both care to join us?"

Glossman held up a hand and shook his head. "Thank you, no, I have some business to tend to."

"I'm afraid I must bow out as well," Blackgaard said.

Whittaker looked genuinely disappointed. "Oh . . .

all right. Well, I guess we'll see you both next week then."

Blackgaard smiled and bowed slightly. "Looking forward to it."

"Yeah," Glossman sneered. "Can't wait."

Blackgaard and Glossman watched the farmer and the soda shop owner head for the chamber's exit. "Well," Glossman muttered, "at least they didn't vote you down."

"No thanks to you," Blackgaard growled. "I thought you wanted to run this town, Philip, but it appears I was mistaken."

Glossman scowled. "I did what I could!"

Blackgaard continued looking at the exit. "Which was practically nothing."

"You saw how difficult it was to fight against Riley!" Glossman hissed. "Especially when Whittaker's here!"

Blackgaard drew in a deep breath. Glossman had a point. He exhaled slowly and murmured, "Yes . . . well, we'll just have to make sure they're not here when we take the vote then, won't we?"

Glossman glanced up at him and then looked away again. "Now wait a minute," he said. "I have to be careful about getting involved in any more of your . . . sinister plans!"

"Who said anything about sinister plans?" Blackgaard replied coolly. "All I want you to do is to tell me what you know about Riley."

"And Whittaker?"

A faint smile curved Blackgaard's lips. "One thing at a time. First, Riley."

Glossman swallowed hard and fumbled nervously with his tie. "Well . . . besides being on the town council, he's also an elder in his church. He's an apple farmer, lives on the outskirts of town. He likes horses—he owned one and just got another and built an addition to his barn for them."

Blackgaard's smile grew wider.

CHAPTER FIVE

Weird.

That was the best word 16-year-old Connie Kendall could find to describe her life at the moment.

She gazed at her reflection in her dresser mirror, fixed her auburn hair into a ponytail, checked the liner on her green, almond-shaped eyes, and then stepped back and sighed heavily. Normally she'd be heading off to work at Whit's End right about now. But since she'd been fired from there at the beginning of the summer, she had no place to go.

That's what was weird. She thought her time at Camp What-A-Nut might make her feel better, but though she had learned quite a bit there about life, leadership, and responsibility, she still felt restless, uncertain, and . . . well, weird. As though there were more she needed to learn.

And then there was Whit.

She'd had no contact with her former boss since her firing, partly because she was up at the camp for much of the time. She also wasn't sure she should contact him. She was still embarrassed and ashamed of the reason he had fired her in the first place, and the look of bitter disappointment in his eyes when he did so haunted her.

But she also knew Whit had a great capacity for forgiveness. She had seen him exercise it over and over again with the kids at Whit's End. Of course, none of them had done anything as bad as she had done.

Connie really did want to see him, maybe even get her job back, but had enough time passed so that she wouldn't seem cloying and anxious? She looked into her reflection's eyes, sighed again, and muttered, "What to do, what to do . . ."

She heard her mom pull out a chair at the kitchen table downstairs, sit, and unfold the morning paper—her daily ritual. A thought struck Connie: *Maybe Mom will have the answer.*

She exited her room and clomped down the stairs and into the kitchen. Sure enough, her mom was engrossed in the *Odyssey Times*, only the top of her head visible from behind the paper.

"Morning, Mom," Connie said.

June Kendall lowered the *Times* and smiled up at her daughter. "Morning, sweetheart," she answered. "You want some breakfast?"

Connie sighed once more and replied wistfully, "No, thank you. I'll just have some juice."

"Okay," June said brightly, disappearing behind the paper again.

Connie frowned. She wanted her mom's advice, but she didn't want to have to *ask* for it. She wanted Mom to understand her dilemma and offer some sage words of counsel. As Whit would.

Connie went to the fridge, retrieved the orange juice, poured herself a glass, replaced the container, and sat at the table across from her mom. She took a sip of the juice, set down the glass, and let out another audible sigh. "Hhhmmm . . ."

June lowered the paper again. "Uh, is something wrong, honey?" she asked.

Her eyes twinkled with amusement, which irked Connie for some reason, so she decided to play the drama for all it was worth. "Hmm? Oh, no . . . nothing's wrong," Connie said. "Go back to your paper, Mom."

The hint of a knowing grin curved June's mouth. She replied, "Thank you," and slowly raised the paper again.

Connie waited for a few seconds and then let loose with the loudest sigh yet: "HHHMMM . . ."

June dropped the paper to the table and fixed her daughter with an irritated stare. "All right, Connie, what's the matter?" she asked.

Connie feigned innocence. "The matter?"

"Yes, 'the matter.' You've been brooding and moping and sighing ever since you got back from camp."

The jab hit home. "I don't think I've been brooding or moping."

"We both know you have. Now, if there's something on your mind, let's get it out in the open."

Connie decided to string her along further. "There's nothing on my mind . . ."

"Nothing you want to talk about?"

"No. Really. You just go back to your paper, Mom."

"Connie—"

"*Really!* It's all right."

June's eyes narrowed, and she slowly raised the *Times* back up in front of her.

Connie waited until the paper got into place, grinned, and said, "Well, since you brought it up . . ."

June immediately closed the paper, refolded it, and put it on the table next to her coffee cup with a chortle. "I knew it! All right, young lady, what's the problem?"

Fun and games were over. It was time for an answer. "Well . . . it's . . . Whit."

June's brow furrowed. "Whit? What about him?"

"I . . . I don't know if I should see him or not."

June's face relaxed into understanding. "Oh. What do you think you should do?"

"I think it'd still hurt to see him again," Connie replied. "I mean, we didn't exactly part under the best of circumstances."

June nodded. "Well, then, you probably *shouldn't* see him."

"But I really *want* to! I mean, some things happened up at camp that I think he'd like to hear about."

"Okay, then, maybe you *should* go see him."

Connie jumped up from her chair. "I don't want to seem pushy!" She paced the floor. "I mean, even though it's been a while, he might not have cooled down yet, and I don't want to do anything that'll bug him."

"Well, then, I guess you *shouldn't* see him."

"But I *have* to! I need to tell him how wrong I was and that I don't blame him for anything!"

"Then go and see him!"

"I can't do that! He fired me!"

June whacked the paper on the table. "Will you cut that out!"

Connie stopped pacing and faced her mom.

"'Yes, I'll see him. No, I won't see him. Yes, I'll see him. No, I won't see him . . .'" June mocked. "I feel like I'm at a tennis match, and I'm the ball!"

Connie sank back into the chair. "Sorry, Mom . . ."

June leaned forward and patted Connie's arm gently. "Look, honey, I know this is difficult for you. I know you like Mr. Whittaker a lot, and I'm sure he feels the same way about you."

"Even though he fired me?"

June nodded. "Yes, even though he fired you. From what I know about him, I don't think he'd do something like that out of spite or unless he had a good reason."

Connie shook her head. "No . . . but that still doesn't tell me what I should do."

"That's because the only one who can tell you what to do is *you*—your heart," June replied. "If you feel it's best to go see him, then *go*—see him, talk to him, get things out in the open. But if you feel that would just make matters worse, then stay away. You may not like this, but there *are* other places to work, you know."

Connie lowered her head. "Yeah," she said softly, "that thought has crossed my mind."

June squeezed Connie's arm affectionately. "Aw, honey, I'm sure you'll make the right decision. And whatever it is, please hurry up and make it before you drive me crazy, huh?" She smiled.

Connie looked up at her mom and giggled. "Okay," she said.

June retrieved the *Odyssey Times* and returned to her reading. Connie watched her and marveled—her mom *did* have the answer after all. Parents could be so surprising at times!

Connie downed the rest of her orange juice, rose, rinsed the glass at the sink, and put it on the dish rack to dry. She'd made a decision. "Um . . . I think I *will* go over to Whit's End," she announced. "Just to take a look around."

June peered at her over the paper. Her eyes twinkled again as she replied, "Mm-hmm."

Connie crossed to June and kissed the top of her head. "Thanks for all your help, Mom," she said. She headed for the front door.

June called after her, "Connie?"

"Yeah?"

"Say hi to Whit for me."

Connie's response was automatic. "Okay, I wi—" She stopped herself. Her mother knew her too well. She smiled and called back in mock frustration, "Mooooom!" She then opened the front door, stepped out, and as she closed it heard her mother's chuckle waft down the hall after her.

CHAPTER SIX

Well, *there's one nice thing about this place,* thought Richard Maxwell. *It's got a lot of great places to hide.*

He was standing in one at the moment, a small alcove just inside the front entrance to Whit's End. From there, he could unobtrusively observe the goings-on in the main room and soda fountain.

There, behind the counter, a lanky, bespectacled, vest-wearing college student served up sodas and dishes of ice cream efficiently to the mob of boisterous children filling the room. Maxwell hadn't seen Eugene Meltsner since they were both fired from Campbell College.

Well, to be accurate, I *was fired and expelled,* Maxwell thought. *Meltsner was transferred back here to finish up his graduate studies under John Whittaker. Working on Applesauce, no doubt.* And that was why Maxwell was here today too.

He noticed that despite the crowd, everyone was polite and patient, and even Meltsner smiled as he worked. Strange. He wouldn't have been so patient. Serving noisy kids was something he would definitely avoid when Blackgaard's Castle opened up.

He was trying to decide how to make his presence known—it was his first time in the place, after all—when the front door opened, the little bell over it jingled, and in walked someone he'd seen before somewhere. She was a cute, young, glasses-wearing brunette about the same age as his half sister, Rachael. In fact, she kind of reminded him of Rachael—and that's why this girl was so familiar. Rachael was friends with Donna

Barclay, who was friends with this girl. But he couldn't remember her name.

Ah, well. It didn't matter. He called to her anyway: "Excuse me, miss?"

She turned and jumped, startled. "Oh! You scared me!" she said.

Time to turn on the charm, he thought. "I'm so sorry! I was wondering if you could help me." He smiled.

Her eyes met his, and her gaze melted. "Um . . . how?"

"I understand there are a lot of machines here— games and the like."

"Yes, I suppose."

"Do you know who maintains them?"

The girl thought for a moment and then replied, "Well, there's Mr. Whittaker, who owns the place. And Eugene, of course." She pointed to him behind the counter.

He raised his hand to scratch his ear, and as he did so, he lightly brushed her arm. "Eugene, yes . . . could you tell him I'd like to talk to him?" He gave her his most charming smile. "Please?"

She gulped, and her face flushed. "Sure," she said in a breathy voice. She backed away a step, nearly stumbled over an umbrella stand, turned, and crossed quickly to Meltsner.

Maxwell retreated to his alcove and watched her go. *Ah, the old charm,* he thought, suppressing a chuckle. *Works every time.*

Despite the noise of the main room, he could just make out the conversation at the counter. Meltsner was just finishing up with a customer as the girl walked up to him. "And sixty cents is your change," he said. "Thank you!"

"Eugene?" the girl said.

"Yes, Lucy?"

Lucy! That *was her name!* A memory of her and Donna visiting the geezers at the Odyssey Retirement Home flashed through Maxwell's mind.

Lucy gestured back in Maxwell's direction. "There's a man over by the front door who wants to see you."

"Me?" Meltsner replied, following her gesture. "Why me?"

"I don't know. He just told me to get the person who fixes the machines."

Meltsner sighed. "Oh, very well . . ." He made his way out from behind the counter and joined Lucy, and together they walked toward him. Their voices got louder as they approached. "He's probably a salesman of some sort. Did he tell you his name?"

"No," Lucy replied. "He's very nice looking, though."

That was Maxwell's cue. He stepped out from the alcove and said, "Well, thank you very much!"

Meltsner's jaw dropped, and he all but jumped backward. "Richard!" he declared.

"Surprise!"

Lucy looked quickly between them, perplexed. "You know each other?" she asked.

Maxwell smirked. "We used to work together. Ain't that right, Meltsy baby?"

Meltsner stiffened. "We were briefly employed by the same organization."

Maxwell chortled. "'We were briefly employed by the

same organization,'" he mocked. "You crack me up!" He turned to Lucy. "We worked with the three Cs."

She frowned. "What's the three Cs?"

"Campbell College computers."

Lucy giggled. "Oh, that's *clever*!"

Maxwell gave her a wink. "Yeah, and *cute*, too!" They both laughed. "Hey, Meltsy, she's all right."

Lucy blushed and giggled again.

Meltsner's face flashed alarm, and he took a protective stance. "Yes . . . uh, Lucy, why don't you go on about your tasks?"

Maxwell leaned toward Lucy and whispered loudly, "He means go have a good time." He looked back up at Meltsner. "Meltsy, babe, you gotta learn to speak English!"

Lucy giggled again.

Meltsner cleared his throat and said curtly, "Run along now, Lucy."

Lucy shot him an annoyed look, huffed, and said, "All right, Eugene." She moved away, then turned back and said sweetly, "Bye, Richard."

Maxwell smiled at her again. "So long, toots!" He gave her another wink.

She sighed dreamily and floated off.

Maxwell watched her go. She really did remind him of Rachael. "Nice kid," he said.

Meltsner stepped in front of him, blocking his view. "Yes, she is—and we'd like her to stay that way."

Maxwell backed up a step. "Oooo! Easy, boy! Why the hostility?"

"I've seen the effect you can have on those younger and weaker than yourself."

"Like little Nicky back at the college?"

"Precisely."

Maxwell grimaced. "Hey, man, cut me some slack! I already paid my debt to society, ya know? They fired me."

"Yes . . ." Meltsner replied skeptically. "Well, is there anything I can help you with, Richard?"

"How formal!" Maxwell scoffed. "Lighten up, will ya? I just came over to see where you're working now." He took a few steps past Meltsner, scanned the main room and soda fountain, and snorted. "So this is the famous Whit's End, huh? Doesn't look like much."

Meltsner sniffed. "There is, to use a colloquialism, much more to it than meets the eye."

Maxwell shrugged. "If you say so. And you got fired from this place because you messed up a computer program—what was it called, uh, Apple Core . . . Banana Peel . . . ?"

"Applesauce, and I didn't 'mess it up.' I simply used it when I wasn't supposed to."

Maxwell smirked, suppressed it, and turned to face Meltsner. "Oh . . . and I suppose it caused all kinds of problems or something?"

"I don't really believe it's any of your business," Meltsner replied coolly.

Maxwell raised his hands. "Okay, okay, take it easy. Man, you're so high strung! I'm only asking 'cause I think it's kinda strange for you to get fired for using a computer program when I don't even see any computers *around* here, that's all."

"As I said, there's more to this establishment than meets the eye."

"I guess so," Maxwell said, nodding. "You know, I use a lot of computers where I'm working now. If you want, I can put in a good word with my boss."

Meltsner shook his head curtly. "Thank you, but I have quite enough intellectual stimulation where I am. Now, if you'll excuse me, I really must clean these tables."

Maxwell snickered.

Meltsner huffed, brushed the hair from his eyes, and headed toward the main room. But he was stopped by the muffled ringing of a phone. He looked in the direction of the ringing—the kitchen—and then back at the dirty tables in the main room. "Oh, dear . . ." he said.

Maxwell inched up beside him. "Hey, you go get the phone, and I'll clear off the tables."

Meltsner glanced at him and looked torn. The phone rang again. "Uh, that won't be necessary—"

Maxwell clapped him on the shoulder. "It's the least

I can do!" The phone rang again. "G'wan, g'wan! You don't want 'em to hang up, do ya?"

Meltsner frowned and then said, "Well, all right." He made his way behind the counter and toward the kitchen's swinging door, calling back as he went, "Just put the dishes in the sink." He pointed to a location behind the counter.

"No problemo!" Maxwell called after him with a wave.

Meltsner frowned, then exited into the kitchen.

Maxwell smiled. *It'll give me a chance to take a look at what's back there*, he thought. He moved quickly to the nearest table, scooped up two syrup-stained sundae dishes, and then followed Eugene's path behind the counter. He wasn't quite sure what he expected to find there, but what immediately greeted him was a disappointment: Two large, horizontal ice cream freezers on rollers sat next to a messy food preparation ledge, complete with rows of sloppy sundae toppings tucked under the top counter. In the middle of the prep ledge was a sink full of dirty dishes.

He scowled, peered farther down the counter, and saw something that looked more promising. At the end, under the cash register, were several small shelves stocked with neat stacks of what appeared to be forms.

He added the dishes he was carrying to the ones in the sink, then crept to the kitchen door to make sure Eugene was still on the phone. Satisfied, he slunk toward the register, glanced around to see if anyone was looking, and then ducked down. He riffled through the papers rapidly. They were forms, all right—inventory forms, ice cream order forms, repair and maintenance forms, and a box of receipts. Nothing helpful.

Maxwell was just about to rise up again when he heard the bell above the front door tinkle and several kids call out greetings:

"Connie!"

"Hi, Connie!"

"It's good to see you!"

"Hey, when are you gonna start workin' here again, Connie?"

A high-pitched, teenaged voice responded, "Hi, guys! It's good to see you all again! Uh, I hope to start back here again soon!"

As she and the kids continued to talk, Maxwell rose up just enough to peer over the counter at her. *So this is the infamous Connie Kendall!* She was a cute high schooler, with a heart-shaped face, green eyes, and brown hair pulled up into a long ponytail, wearing a green blouse and surrounded by kids.

He sank down again and considered how to play this. He knew Connie had been fired the same day Meltsner had, but she didn't know that he knew. And Meltsner was working here again and she wasn't—though it sounded as if she *wanted* to. He smirked. *There may be an opportunity here*, he thought. *At the very least, I can have a little fun.*

She had stopped talking with the brats and was mumbling to herself as she left them and approached the counter. He could just make out what she was saying: "Well, at least the kids want me back. I wonder who's here . . ." She called out, "Hello?"

That was his signal. He popped up, feigning fright. "Wha—?"

She jumped and barked out, "Oh!"

Maxwell put his hand on his chest and gulped a deep breath. "Don't sneak up on people like that!" he said. "You could give a guy a heart attack!"

"I'm sorry! I—I didn't see you back there!" Her expression changed instantly from startled to worried. "Are—are you the new employee?"

He stifled a smile. "Me? You gotta be kidding!"

Now she went from worry to suspicion. "You don't work here? Then why are you behind the counter?"

He shrugged. "I'm just helping out the guy who *does*. He's on the phone back in the kitchen."

He had timed it perfectly. At that moment, the kitchen door swung open and Meltsner entered. "All right, Richard, thank you for your help," he said, "but I can handle—"

Connie's look was exactly what Maxwell hoped for: shock, hurt, and anger. Her jaw dropped. "Eugene!"

And for an added bonus, Meltsner looked completely

nonplussed. "M-Miss Kendall!" he stammered. "Uh, hello!"

It was all Maxwell could do to keep from busting out laughing.

CHAPTER SEVEN

"How touching," Maxwell said with a smirk. "I take it you two know each other?"

Meltsner fumbled with his vest. "Uh, yes. Connie Kendall, this is Richard Maxwell. Uh, Miss Kendall and I, uh—"

"I used to work here, but then Eugene and I were both fired," she cut in flatly.

Maxwell's eyebrows rose. "Oh?"

Connie ignored him and glared at Meltsner. "I didn't know you were working here again."

Meltsner swallowed hard. "Uh, yes . . . Mr. Whittaker rehired me a fortnight ago."

Maxwell leaned toward Connie and muttered, "That means a couple of weeks."

"I know what it means," she snapped.

Meltsner tugged at his shirt collar and took a deep breath. "Miss Kendall, I know this may look suspicious to you, but there is a logical and rational story behind my rehiring."

Connie held up a hand, cutting him off. "You don't have to explain anything to me, Eugene," she said quietly. "This is Whit's business. He can hire whomever he wants."

Maxwell could barely keep his composure. Inside, he was jumping up and down with glee at the discomfort he was witnessing.

It grew even worse a moment later when Lucy ran up and said, "Eugene—" She all but froze when she saw

Connie, and her sweet voice turned Arctic cold. "Oh. Connie. It's you."

Connie shifted her weight from one foot to the other. "Yeah . . . hi, Lucy," she murmured.

Interesting, thought Maxwell, his gaze shifting between them.

Meltsner piped up: "What is it this time, Lucy?"

"Something's wrong with the Noah's Ark display in the Bible Room," she answered. "The lions are mooing, and the cows are barking."

Meltsner turned to Maxwell, eyes narrowing with suspicion. "Really?" Meltsner asked.

Maxwell said with a shrug, "Hey, don't look at me! I've been right here behind the counter since you left!"

"Hmph," Meltsner grunted. "Very well, I shall examine it. I'll return shortly, so . . . everyone, please refrain from touching anything." He gave them each a quick but stern glance, lingering a bit on Connie, and then huffed and headed up the staircase.

No one said anything for a long moment, and the

tension between Lucy and Connie was thicker than molasses on a freezing day.

Oh, this is too delicious! thought Maxwell, suppressing a grin. *And here I thought this trip would be for nothing! What is going on between* these *two?* Aloud he muttered, "Somebody tell a joke or something . . ."

Connie forced a smile and said lightly, "So, Lucy, how ya doin'?"

Lucy looked straight ahead, her voice still icy. "Fine."

Connie took a breath and tried again. "I haven't seen you since you got back from camp."

Now Lucy slowly turned and glared daggers at her. "That's 'cause I've been on restriction."

Connie's face flushed, and she stared at the floor. "Oh," she said quietly.

Lucy pressed on, getting heated. "Yeah, my parents were very upset that I was sent home early. So they grounded me."

Connie met her gaze, sympathy in her eyes. "I'm sorry, Lucy, but . . . I had to send you home. You said you understood."

Lucy looked away again. "I thought I did, but now I'm not so sure. It's one thing to get into trouble when you do something wrong, but when you get in trouble for trying to keep somebody *else* from doing wrong—"

"Lucy, we went over this at camp," Connie interrupted. "You *did* do something wrong! You broke one of the rules—*twice*, in fact."

"It was a stupid rule," Lucy muttered.

"Lucy—"

"You didn't have to send me home, Connie. You could've given me another chance."

"When you break the rules, you have to suffer the consequences! That's why Eugene and I got fired—because we broke the rules!"

Lucy crossed her arms. "Then how come Eugene is working here again?" she said cattily.

Connie took a breath. "I—I don't know . . ."

"Because Mr. Whittaker gave him another chance," Lucy answered, leaning forward slightly. "Mr. Whittaker knows what *compassion* means."

Oooo! Knockout punch! Maxwell thought. *That one* really *hurt!*

Connie withered visibly, to the point where he almost felt sorry for her.

Time to step in and play referee. Maxwell pulled on an imaginary cord and made a sound like a boxing bell. "Ding, ding, ding! End of round one!" he said jovially. "Maybe you should both go to neutral corners and cool off!"

Lucy's arms dropped to her sides, and her back stiffened. "I don't have to cool off, but going away sounds like a good idea. See you later, Richard." She tromped away.

Connie turned and called after her. "Lucy!" But the younger girl was already halfway up the stairs. Connie's shoulders drooped. "Oh, Lucy . . ."

Maxwell gave it a moment, then said softly, "She was pretty mad, huh?"

"Yeah. I didn't know she felt that way. I thought everything was all right."

Push it a bit, he thought. "She really let you have it with that crack about Eugene and Whittaker."

Connie sighed. "Yeah, well, she was mad. She didn't know what she was saying."

And a bit more. "Maybe . . . then again, you know the old saying: 'Out of the mouths of babes . . .'"

Connie turned to face him. "What are you talking about?"

"Nothing," he replied innocently. "Just that . . . there may be more truth to Lucy's statement than you think."

"Like what?"

Careful! "Well . . . there must be *some* reason Whittaker hired ol' Meltsnerd while you were at camp . . ." *Now—plant the idea.* "Maybe he's playing favorites."

Connie's head snapped back, and she scowled. "No way! Whit's not like that!"

He nodded casually. "If you say so . . . But you gotta admit, both of you were working here, then both of you got fired, and then Whittaker hires *Eugene* back while you're out of town? Sounds pretty weird to me."

She shook her head. It was obvious the thought had occurred to her, but she was fighting it. "You . . . you don't know what you're talking about, so . . . why don't you just be quiet."

He shrugged again. "Hey, it's none of my business. But if I were you, I'd definitely consider my alternatives." *Time to reel her in.* "After all, Whit's End isn't the only place in town to work, you know."

She looked almost startled. "Yeah," she muttered, "that's what my mom said too." She blinked and stared at him for an instant as though she had never seen him before. Then recognition returned to her expression, and she stammered, "Um, i-it was nice meeting you . . ." and headed for the front door.

Oh, no, you're not getting away that *easily,* he thought. Aloud he said, "Leaving? I was about to go too. I'll come with you."

He sidled up next to her, his mind racing. If he could get Connie Kendall to join them—*What a coup! She could tell us all sorts of things about this place—and Whittaker, too! And maybe it'll make Blackgaard forget about the other stuff he wants me to do.*

They were almost at the front door when it opened,

the bell above it tinkled, and in walked the man himself: John Avery Whittaker, and right behind him, Tom Riley. *This keeps getting better and better!* thought Maxwell.

Riley's face broke out in a big smile. "Well, looky who's here!" he said. He stepped forward and clasped Connie's hand, shaking it heartily.

Connie greeted him warmly: "Hi, Tom."

Whittaker was also smiling. "Connie!" he said. He looked as though he wanted to hug her.

But once Riley dropped her hand, Connie remained still. If anything, she became even more reserved. She nodded slightly and said simply, "Whit."

They all looked at each other awkwardly for a few moments, then Riley piped up again. "It sure is good to see you back here, Connie! This place has been mighty empty without you."

Connie smiled. "It's good to see you both again too."

Whittaker shifted his gaze from Connie to Maxwell. He frowned and said, "Richard."

Maxwell smirked. "You remembered. I'm flattered."

Connie's eyebrows rose. "You know each other?"

"Oh, yeah." Maxwell nodded. "We met at the college a couple of weeks ago." *Time to beat a hasty retreat,* he thought, and aloud he said, "Well, I'm sure you all have a lot to talk about, so I'll just make my adieu."

He moved past the others to the front door, opened it, and stepped outside. He immediately squatted and pressed himself against the door, straining to hear their conversation. He could barely make out what they were saying.

"Nice feller," Riley drawled.

Whittaker grunted. "Hmph. I wonder what he was doing here."

"I think he was visiting Eugene," Connie replied. "He said they knew each other." She cleared her throat softly and continued nervously, "Um, speaking of Eugene . . . I noticed he's working here again."

"Yes, he is," Whittaker said evenly.

There was a pause. Maxwell pressed his ear against the door harder.

Riley again broke the silence. "Were you planning on working somewhere this summer, Connie?" he asked.

"Maybe . . ." she answered. "I've already worked at Camp What-A-Nut."

"Did you have a good time up there?"

"Yeah. I learned a lot."

"Really?" Whittaker said, suddenly sounding very interested.

But Connie sounded even more subdued. "Yeah . . . and I've learned a lot since I've been back, too." Another pause, then she added, "Listen, I'd better be going—"

Maxwell jumped up, vaulted off the porch and down the front steps, and crouched behind a bush alongside the building. He had barely made it when the front door opened and Connie stepped outside, closing it behind her. She stopped there for a moment, looked back at the door longingly, and then turned and strode off the porch and down the sidewalk.

Maxwell smiled, then jumped up and followed her. When they were near the street, he quickened his pace and sidled up next to her. "Hey!" he greeted her.

She started slightly, frowned at him, and said, "Oh, it's you."

They kept walking.

"Uh-oh. I take it Whittaker didn't offer you your job back?" Maxwell asked.

"No, he didn't."

Excellent! "Aw, that's too bad. That happens to friends sometimes."

She swallowed hard. "Yeah, I know."

He reached out and grasped her arm softly, stopping her. He channeled every ounce of sympathy he had into his expression. "Listen," he said gently, "like I said before, Whit's End isn't the only place in town to work, you know. I could introduce you to my boss . . . if you're interested."

She looked at his hand on her arm and then up at his face for a long moment. He could almost hear the war going on inside her mind. Her face was a study in anguish. Then, like the sun breaking through the clouds after a storm, determination replaced the anguish.

This is it! he thought.

She nodded slowly, took a deep breath, and said, "All right. Let's go."

Chapter Eight

"**H**ere we are!" Maxwell announced.

He opened the front doors of Blackgaard's Castle, made way for Connie to enter ahead of him, followed her in, and then closed the doors behind them.

Connie frowned. "This is where you work?" she asked skeptically. "It's an empty building. Didn't it used to be a computer store?"

"Along with other small businesses," Maxwell replied, nodding. "My boss bought it all, gutted it, and is rebuilding it from the foundation up! See? You're getting in on the ground floor of a brand-new operation!"

"Where are all the workers?"

Maxwell shrugged. "I dunno—lunch, probably."

Connie licked her lips nervously. "Uh, I don't know about this."

"I'm tellin' ya, this is a great opportunity!" He patted her arm. "Listen, you just stay here, and let me go get the boss. He'll explain everything to you." He bounded across the room and disappeared behind a door marked "Private."

Connie watched him go and muttered, "This is weird." She took a few tentative steps into the spacious room, scrutinizing it cautiously.

The place wasn't really empty but a work in progress. Wires hung from the ceiling and draped the walls. Stacks of lumber, pallets of drywall, huge spools of electrical wire, and other building supplies sat in random places around the space. Enormous upright, misshapen boxes, covered with tied-down tarpaulins, were also scattered around the room. In the dim and shadowy light, the boxes seemed like captured ogres or trolls who a moment before had been strolling around the room and then squatted and turned to stone a split second before she and Maxwell entered. Only when she saw "Zappazoids" written across the bottom of one box did she realize they were arcade video games.

Despite them and the building materials, the space was still empty enough that voices and footsteps echoed off the barren walls. Connie shivered and was just getting ready to leave when the "Private" door opened and Maxwell reappeared, followed by a tall, angular, handsome man with jet-black hair that was streaked with white at the temples and a neatly clipped Vandyke on his chin, wearing an immaculate three-piece suit. A large, fluffy, gray cat also darted out the door and disappeared behind the huge boxes.

Maxwell and the man strode across the room to her, and the closer they got, the taller the man seemed and the more unnerved Connie felt. Maxwell was all smiles. "Here he is, Connie," he said. "Boss, I want you to meet Connie Kendall. Connie, this is my boss."

The man stepped forward and extended his hand. "How do you do, Miss Kendall?" his rich baritone intoned. "My name is Blackgaard."

Connie took his hand, gave it a quick shake, and dropped it. "Hello, Mr. Blackgaard," she replied.

"That's *Doctor* Blackgaard, Connie," Maxwell cut in.

"Oh, I'm sorry. Are you into medicine?"

Blackgaard shook his head. "No, I'm a PhD."

Maxwell jumped in again. "He's an expert on kids."

Connie's eyebrows rose. "Really?"

"I know something about them," Blackgaard responded with a smile. "So, Miss Kendall, Richard tells me you're looking for employment?"

"Well . . . maybe."

"Only maybe?"

She shrugged. "Uh, well . . . yeah, I guess I am."

Blackgaard gestured grandly around the room. "I may have a position for you here at Blackgaard's Castle, once it opens."

Connie gazed around the room once again. "That's what you're gonna call this place—Blackgaard's Castle?"

Maxwell wagged his eyebrows. "Yeah—pretty radical, huh?"

Connie managed a weak smile. "Uh . . . yeah . . . radical."

Blackgaard leaned casually against a pallet of drywall sheets. The cat jumped up on them and sat next to him. He stroked the cat's neck absently and said, "So, Connie, why don't you tell me about yourself, your background?"

Connie took a breath. "Well . . . I'm 16 . . . I've lived in Odyssey for almost two years now . . . uh . . . I go to Odyssey High . . . um . . . I'm really active in my church . . ."

"What about your employment experience?" Blackgaard asked. "Have you ever worked with children before?"

Maxwell snorted. "Are you kidding?" he said. "I told you she worked for—"

Blackgaard stopped stroking the cat. "If you don't mind, Richard," he interrupted curtly, "I'd like to hear it from her." His coal-black eyes snapped but never stopped looking at Connie.

Maxwell cleared his throat and stepped back. "Oh . . . uh, yeah. Sorry."

Blackgaard resumed stroking the cat and nodded for Connie to continue.

She licked her lips nervously. "Well, like Richard was about to tell you, I used to work at Whit's End, across town."

"Used to? You don't work there anymore?"

She dropped her gaze to the floor. "No."

"What happened?" Blackgaard asked gently.

"I was . . . fired."

"I see. May I ask why?"

She sighed heavily. "Well, it's kinda complicated. I sort of used a computer program I wasn't supposed to use."

Maxwell piped up. "You mean Applesauce?"

Connie's head jerked up, and she blinked. "Yeah! How'd you know?"

Maxwell smiled wanly. "Eugene told me."

Blackgaard picked up the cat, which purred contentedly. "You say you 'sort of' used it?"

Her gaze returned to the floor. "Yeah . . . I . . . I just wanted to see how it worked. I don't know anything about computers, but I guess I accidentally did the right thing, 'cause before I knew what was happening, it started up."

Blackgaard's brow furrowed. "So you were fired for being curious?"

She shook her head slightly. "Well, not exactly. I wasn't supposed to be in the computer room in the first place. In fact, I wasn't even supposed to know there *was* a computer room."

Blackgaard pondered her words for a moment. "It still sounds like you were fired for simply being curious. That's terribly unjust. I don't blame you for being upset."

Connie looked up at him quickly. "Oh, I'm not upset. I don't think it's unjust, either. If Whit—I mean, Mr. Whittaker—wanted me to know about the computer room, he would have told me. He trusted me, and I let him down."

Maxwell had moved around behind her so quietly

she jumped when she heard his voice. "Sounds kinda paranoid to me," he said, "keepin' all sorts of secrets like that, I mean."

She whirled to face him. "He is *not* paranoid!"

Blackgaard stood. "No, of course not, Richard," he said smoothly. "Obviously this Applesauce is a very special program."

Connie turned back to him. "That's right! That's what Whit said."

Blackgaard smiled and nodded. "Yes . . ." He leaned slightly toward her. "Do you . . . remember what it did?" he asked offhandedly.

She looked down again and cocked her head to one side. "Well, it . . . it—" She stopped suddenly and looked back and forth between them.

Blackgaard still leaned toward her, smiling benignly. The cat also gazed at her from the crook of his arm. But Maxwell stared at her hungrily and was leaning so far forward he seemed about to topple over. "What?" he whispered insistently. "It *what?*"

Connie backed up a few steps, swallowed hard, and

said, "I . . . I don't see what that has to do with my getting a job here."

For a long moment everyone stood immobile. Blackgaard still gazed calmly and steadily at Connie, but her eyes darted between him, the cat, and Maxwell, while Maxwell glanced at Blackgaard and then back at her.

Finally Blackgaard smiled widely and stood up straight. "You're quite right, Connie," he said disarmingly, "quite right. Forgive our questions. The only reason we ask is because Blackgaard's Castle will also employ computers, the very latest in technology. And, naturally, we're curious about any new programs that may come along. You understand."

She exhaled. "Uh, yeah, I understand."

Maxwell had also backed off, shrugged, and smiled charmingly. "Yeah, it's just curiosity."

Blackgaard leaned up against the stack of drywall again and set the cat back on it. "Well, Connie," he said, "I must say I am impressed. If you'd like to work here at Blackgaard's Castle, I can certainly find a spot for you."

Maxwell rubbed his hands together. "Hey, that's great!" he said.

Connie smiled graciously. "Uh, well, I don't want to appear ungrateful, but could I have some time to think about it?"

"Of course!" Blackgaard said with a nod. Then he held up a finger and added, "But I'd advise you to give your answer quickly, because we'll be starting business here within the next few weeks."

Maxwell gave her forearm a gentle squeeze. "It'll be great working with you, Connie!"

She looked at his hand, then at his face, and then at Blackgaard's. The cat peered around him at her. "Yeah . . . well . . . I'll let you know as soon as I can." She turned and walked to the front doors. Once there, she turned back and waved. "Good-bye."

"Good-bye!"

"So long!"

They watched her exit through the doors. Maxwell was about to say something when Blackgaard held up a hand to stop him. They both moved stealthily to the front doors. Blackgaard opened one slightly and peered out. Connie was running from the building as fast as her legs could carry her. Blackgaard stifled a chuckle, closed the door, and moved back into the room.

Maxwell followed him. "So whaddya think?" he asked. "You gonna hire her?"

"No. Whittaker's hold over her is too great. However, she may still be useful for our immediate purposes."

Maxwell nodded. "Getting Whittaker out of the way for the vote."

"Yes. But it must be done carefully so they don't suspect anything."

"I think that can be arranged," Maxwell said, smirking.

Blackgaard returned his smirk with one of his own. "That's why I hired you . . . excellent. And what about Tom Riley? Are the plans in motion?"

Maxwell's face fell. Blackgaard hadn't forgotten after all. "Uh . . . n-not exactly . . ." He turned and took a few steps away from his boss. "I mean . . . I'm not so sure about it . . . I mean, manipulating kids is one thing, but . . . that's *too* much."

There was a long pause. Suddenly Blackgaard's deep voice growled with a hostility Maxwell had never heard from him before: "You silly little sniveling coward."

Maxwell whipped around, stunned. "W-wha—?"

What he saw coming turned his surprise to terror. Blackgaard all but charged at him, face red with fury, lips curled into a snarl. "You dare even *think* about disobeying my orders? Just remember, my fine young man, that I hold your future. We both know you're guilty of far worse acts than changing the grades of a few eggheads at the college. Perhaps you'd like me to pick up the phone and tell the authorities about them!"

The ferocity of Blackgaard's attack caught Maxwell completely off guard. He backed up against the Zappazoids game, colliding with it hard, bumping his head against its side and nearly toppling it. Sasha screeched and scrambled for cover and safety. Blackgaard towered over Maxwell, teeth gritted and bared, nostrils flared, one hand clutching Maxwell's shirt, the other raised in a fist.

There was no time to conjure a clever verbal comeback. All Maxwell could manage was to hold up his arms in front of his face defensively and whimper a meek "N-no, please!"

And suddenly, Blackgaard's visage returned to normal, as though his outburst of fury had been a passing summer shower. He lowered his fist, released his grip on Maxwell's shirt, and smoothed out the wrinkles in it. His voice was once again silky smooth. "That's better," he said. "You're a smart fellow, Richard. I'm going to need people like you to help me run this town—and for even bigger things. Just make sure you don't let me down."

Maxwell trembled, and it took everything in him to stop it. For a moment he thought he would pass out. But he finally regained control and whispered, "I-I won't."

The incident was evoking in him memories he had long suppressed, and he didn't like it. He rubbed the back of his head gingerly, winced, sank to the floor, and then glared up at Blackgaard with a deep frown.

Blackgaard chuckled, then patted him on the cheek.

"Oh, don't have such a long face! This should be a lot of fun for you, Richard! After all, it's not everyone who gets to ruin two of Odyssey's most powerful men at the same time." He threw back his head and laughed loud, long, and deep, then turned and headed back to the "Private" door, calling out, "Sasha!"

The cat emerged from between two of the huge boxes and loped across the room to join him. They both disappeared behind the door, leaving Maxwell huddled against the game, shaking.

CHAPTER NINE

"Tom, she's beautiful!"

John Avery Whittaker stood in Tom Riley's barn, scratching and patting the long, sturdy, brown-and-white neck of an Appaloosa mare. The morning sunshine poured through the barn's open door, and a soft breeze brought the occasional and faint whiff of apples from the acres of orchards outside.

The pony nickered and pressed her soft lips against Whit's other arm, sniffing for more sugar cubes. He obliged, fishing them out of his jacket pocket. "There you go," he murmured softly. As the pony nibbled them, he cooed, "Oh, my, you're a good girl, aren't you? Yes, you are."

Tom finished breaking up a bale of hay at the far end of the barn and observed Whit and the pony with a smile. "Yeah, I'm pretty pleased with her," he said.

"What'd you name her?"

"Rachel."

Whit rubbed Rachel's nose gently. "You're a real beauty, Rachel!"

There was a sudden and very loud whinny, followed by a gentle nudge against Whit's shoulder from the American paint mare in the next stall. Whit turned and chuckled. "Oh ho, Leah!" he said. "Sneakin' up on me, eh?"

Tom laughed. "She's still a little jealous."

Whit fished in his pocket for more sugar. "Don't worry, I have some for you, too." He held out the cubes in his flattened palm, and Leah scooped them into her mouth and crunched them contentedly. Whit patted both horses. "So now you have Leah and Rachel, just like in the Bible."

Tom speared a forkful of hay and lugged it over to Leah's stall. "Yeah. It was my wife's idea." He plopped the hay into the feed trough just inside the gate.

"Where is Agnes anyway?" asked Whit.

Tom retrieved another forkful of hay and brought it to Rachel's stall. "She went to visit her sister back East. She'll be gone for a couple of weeks."

"Oh." Both horses now turned their attention to the hay. "Well, I'd say you have two fine horses here, Mr. Riley. They seem to be very open and trusting."

Tom retrieved two salt licks on ropes from a storage bin and crossed to Leah's stall. "Yeah," he sighed, tying one lick onto the inside of the gate. "If only people were like that."

Whit chuckled. "Now, *that's* a cue for a conversation if I ever heard one!"

Tom also chuckled. "Guess it was pretty obvious." He tied the second lick onto Rachel's stall gate.

"You worried about the vote tomorrow?"

"Yeah," Tom said, nodding. "I don't know about this Blackgaard feller. I guess I shouldn't be so hard on him, but I just find it suspicious that he won't tell us what he wants to do with his place."

Whit upended a large pail and sat on it. "Well, for what it's worth, I think you handled it the right way. You're certainly right to be concerned, and you're trying to be fair."

Tom put his foot on the bottom rail of Rachel's stall and rested his arm on the top rail. "Tell that to Glossman." He shook his head. "I declare, he's the most argumentative man I ever met!"

Whit chuckled again. "You and he do seem to butt heads quite a bit."

"Yeah, but I'm not sure I'm gonna come out on top this time. This vote could go either way. You're gonna be there, aren't you?"

"I sure plan to," Whit said. "Right beside you all the way."

"Good," Tom sighed, "'cause I'm gonna need all the help I can get. I just hope it's enough."

Whit leaned back against a post. "Remember what

David said when he went up against Goliath: 'The battle is the Lord's.' You need to put it in His hands and trust that He'll do what's best."

"Yeah . . ." Tom stroked his chin for a moment. "Y'know, John Avery, that sounds like a piece of advice you might want to apply to yourself."

Whit's brow furrowed. "What do you mean?"

"Does the name Connie Kendall ring a bell?"

Whit lowered his gaze. "Mmm . . . I guess *that's* pretty obvious too."

Tom nodded. "Uh-huh. Have you talked with her again since you last saw her?"

"No . . . and that worries me."

"Why?"

Whit sat up. "Because the last time I saw her, she was with Richard Maxwell. I told you about what he did at the college, didn't I?"

"Mmm-hmm—makin' that little boy change all those grades."

"Yes. Eugene said Maxwell was talking to Connie before we came in the other day."

Tom plucked a piece of loose straw from his shirt. "You think that's why she left so sudden?" He stuck the straw in the corner of his mouth.

Whit shook his head. "I don't know." He leaned forward, picked up a halter from the ground, and began absently unbuckling and then rebuckling the crownpiece.

Tom turned and half sat on one of the gate rails. "Whit, why did you let her leave yesterday? Why didn't you give her her job back then and there?"

"She didn't ask for it back," Whit said quietly. "She has to ask for it back."

"Don't you think you're being too harsh on her?"

Whit stopped fiddling with the halter and looked at Tom. "Let me ask you something: Why didn't you agree to grant Dr. Blackgaard a license at the town council meeting last week?"

Tom straightened up. "Well, like I said, I didn't know what kind of business he wants to start. I need more information about it."

Whit nodded. "Well, I need more information

about Connie. See, I could hire Eugene back because I knew he understood why I fired him in the first place. He had an experience that *taught* him. But I can't say that about Connie. I don't know if she understands or not." He started fiddling again. "And now if she's associating with Richard Maxwell . . . who knows what he's capable of? I don't like to judge people, but he didn't have the least bit of remorse about what he made Nicholas do. And with Connie in the frame of mind she's in . . . well, it just worries me, that's all."

Tom rose, crossed to Whit, and took the halter from him. "I think Connie has more strength than you're givin' her credit for," he said. He hung the halter on a hook near the barn door.

Whit leaned back again. "Maybe . . . and maybe firing her wasn't such a good idea."

Tom turned back to him and plucked the straw from his mouth. "Now, John Avery, you don't really believe that, do you?"

"No," Whit sighed. "I don't see how I could have handled it any other way."

"You can't back out now. You need to stick to your guns." Tom spat on the floor and replaced the straw in the corner of his mouth.

Whit closed his eyes. "I know," he said wearily. "And when she's ready, I'll be there for her. Until then . . . all I can do is wait."

Tom crossed to his friend and gripped his shoulder firmly but gently. Whit looked up at him. "You're doin' what you believe is right, John Avery. You have to have faith that God'll honor that. Now, I seem to recall somebody just a minute ago saying something about putting things in the Lord's hands and trusting He'll do what's best."

Whit smiled. "You're right, my friend." He rose and turned the pail right side up. "Looks like we could *both* use a little prayer action."

Tom removed the straw and flicked it away. "Now, that's the best idea I've heard all day."

Leah and Rachel, who had long since finished their breakfasts and were once again at their stall gates, looking at the two men, picked that moment to whinny together loudly. Tom grinned. "And it seems I'm not the only one who thinks so!"

Both horses nickered and bobbed their heads. Whit and Tom chuckled.

CHAPTER TEN

That afternoon found Richard Maxwell sitting in a secluded booth at Whit's End. He was still a bit shaken by Blackgaard's outburst yesterday, and especially by his own reaction to it. It was the first time since he began working with Blackgaard that he'd felt truly scared by him—scared and out of control—*even when Blackgaard had Glossman kidnap me*, he thought.

The last time he'd felt so out of control was when he was a boy, after his folks divorced and his mother took up with Osgood Brownlow. At least, that was the name he was going by when he entered their lives all those years ago.

Maxwell leaned back in the booth, closed his eyes, and grimaced at the memory. They were living in Millsburg, and his father, Mickey, was a very smart man, one of the early computer wonks. Turns out he was more interested in his work than he was in his young family, so much so that Richard's mother, Melissa, decided they'd be better off without him. So she took him and his sister, Rachael, moved them all into an apartment, and filed for divorce.

Once it was finalized and she got custody of the children, Mickey moved to Chicago, and Melissa went back to her maiden name: Woodworth. That was when Brownlow came along. *I was what? About ten? Yeah, and Rachael was two.* Melissa never married Brownlow, but he was a regular presence in their lives over the next several years.

He liked Brownlow at first. The gent took care of them financially, had a funny way of talking, and laughed when Richard would charm and flatter his mother out of extra snacks, cookies, candy, and even money. Brownlow told him he had a real talent for smooth talking, and he taught him games and fake-outs to fool his friends.

Only when Maxwell got a little older did he realize that the games and fake-outs were actually cons and scams. When asked about them, Brownlow called them "survival tools." He told Maxwell, "A man's gotta survive, don't he?"

Not that I actually minded scamming kids out of money, Maxwell thought with a smirk. His family needed it, and he also was pleased to learn that he was good at cons—*very* good. And so everyone got along, at least for a while.

Then, about five years into this arrangement, things fell apart. As he got better and better at scamming, and more money came in, Brownlow started demanding a cut of it, which he hadn't done before. When Maxwell balked, Brownlow threatened to tell Melissa what he had been doing.

When Maxwell counterthreatened to tell his mother that Brownlow had been behind it all, Brownlow reacted in much the same way Blackgaard had yesterday. He backed Maxwell into a corner and said in a deadly quiet voice, "Better think twice about that, lad. It'd be a shame if someone you cared about got hurt." Then he backed away and laughed. "On second thought, go ahead and tell her. Who do you think she'll believe?"

Much as he'd hated to admit it, Maxwell suspected Brownlow was right. Melissa would undoubtedly take his word over her own son's.

Maxwell's suspicion was confirmed a few weeks later. On his way home from school one afternoon, he saw Brownlow walking downtown with a woman who was definitely not Melissa. He followed the two discreetly. They went to a pawnshop and walked inside. Maxwell sneaked up to the window and saw what Brownlow and his companion were pawning: several pieces of Melissa's jewelry. Once the transaction was complete, Brownlow gave the money to the woman, who hugged and kissed him.

Maxwell raced home and told his mother about it. As predicted, she accused him of lying. But he had proof. They went to her bedroom and looked in her jewelry box. It was nearly empty. She still didn't believe him.

They went down to the pawnshop, and Maxwell demanded to see the jewelry. The broker produced it. Surely *this* would convince her Brownlow was no good.

But it didn't.

Incredibly, she still sided with Brownlow. She accused her son of stealing and pawning the jewelry just to make Brownlow look bad. She didn't even believe the pawnbroker when he said he'd never seen Maxwell before. They were all lying, she said, all trying to destroy her happiness.

Maxwell winced at the memory. Though he had suspected the truth, when it was actually confirmed, it hit him like a punch to the gut. His mother loved the scoundrel she had brought into their lives more than she loved her own boy.

They walked home from the pawnshop in silence.

Rachael was at a friend's house, and Brownlow was nowhere to be seen. Maxwell packed his things and strode out of the house without a word. Melissa made no effort to stop him. He went to the bus station and took the next bus to his father's place in the Windy City. He was 15. *I never even told Rachael good-bye.*

Maxwell sighed. Despite living in the same apartment over the next three years, the only real interaction he had with his father was when Mickey taught him about computers. Maxwell quickly realized his father was a genius in the subject, and he was pleasantly surprised at his own aptitude for it. He actually understood what his father was talking about when it came to information technology. It didn't make up for Mickey's almost complete lack of affection and closeness—*but, hey, at least I got another "survival tool" out of it, right?*

He smiled again. He had graduated early from high school and, thanks to his father's tutelage, progressed rapidly through the computer science courses at the local community college.

He was bored, though, and in need of cash, so he

began scamming again. He also got a series of odd jobs to supplement the income from his cons. There was always something to do in Chicago—busboy, pizza delivery, janitor, and he even did a stint on the maintenance crew for the sanitation department. He hated it, but he learned how to get around through a bunch of service doors down in the sewers, which could come in handy if he ever needed to move about without being seen.

He also met Greg Kelly in the sanitation department. Greg, he learned, had actually told Blackgaard about him in the first place. *If I ever see him again, I'll have to give him a special "thank-you" for that.*

Then on the morning after his eighteenth birthday, Maxwell woke up to find that Mickey had left. No note, no good-bye, just . . . gone.

Only when Maxwell's computer said, "You've got mail!" and he accessed his e-mail account did he learn where Mickey went. His father had taken a job someplace in the Far East, the missive said, and he didn't know when or even *if* he'd be back.

Mickey explained that he had prepaid his son's

tuition at Campbell College in a place called Odyssey. They had an excellent information technology department, and Maxwell could benefit greatly from it and the rest of his formal education as well. His father had also provided a stipend for living expenses, though Maxwell would have to get a job to supplement it.

Additionally, the missive said, Odyssey was just a few hours from Millsburg, in case he should want to visit his mother and sister. And that was how the e-mail ended, without so much as a good-bye. *Only slightly less affectionate than he was in person*, Maxwell thought.

The last thing he wanted was to move closer to his mother, but seeing Rachael again held some appeal. And since both his jobs and his scamming opportunities were drying up where he was . . . and his education was paid for . . . and he would have some spending money, he decided to give small-town living another try. The following morning he was on a bus, Odyssey-bound.

Much to his surprise, he actually liked the place. It was friendlier than he remembered Millsburg being and far less hectic than Chicago.

His father was right about Campbell College's IT program. It was great, and he learned a lot. He found an inexpensive place off campus to live in, and he had all new victims for his cons and scams. In no time, he had hooked up with some of Odyssey's seedier characters, like Myron "Jellyfish" Horowitz, and started using his other "survival tools" around town as well, in places like the Odyssey Retirement Home. All in all, life was pretty good . . .

. . . for about six months. That was when a surprise showed up on his doorstep: Melissa and Rachael. Brownlow had abandoned them—*ran off after a bigger scam, no doubt*, Maxwell thought. *Probably even changed his name.*

To say things were awkward would be a gross understatement. Over the next year, he and Melissa tried to get along, but their previous unpleasantness, her aloofness, and Rachael's misbehavior kept getting in the way. It was apparent that Brownlow had taught his sister the same games and fake-outs he'd taught him, only she wasn't very good at them. Rather than try to scam or con or finesse, Rachael just took and did whatever she wanted. She kept getting into trouble, and she wouldn't listen to anything he or their mother said.

Then earlier that year, things went from bad to worse: Melissa ran off as well. He never knew where. All she said in the note she left was that she'd needed to find a new life. She ended the note with "Take care of Rachael."

Maxwell sighed. *I tried, I honestly did!* But with their mother gone, Rachael really went off the deep end and became virtually uncontrollable. He thought she might calm down when she befriended Donna Barclay, and for a few weeks Donna's niceness seemed to rub off on her. But then they had a falling-out, and Donna broke off their friendship.

Despite his warnings and threats, Rachael went and got herself arrested—again—for shoplifting. And since there was no actual parent in their home, she was sent to juvenile hall.

He scowled at the bitter taste of bile these recollections erupted in him: disgust for his folks for dumping their responsibility for Rachael on him, loathing for Brownlow for corrupting her, and hatred for himself for not fighting to stay and at least try to protect her.

A thought struck him, and his eyes snapped open. Yesterday, he had tried to help Blackgaard do to Connie what Brownlow had done to Rachael—take a completely innocent girl and corrupt her. And here he was, in Whit's End, about to do it again! How had he not seen this?

He couldn't let it happen—he wouldn't. But Blackgaard had shown yesterday that he was not a man to be denied. And Blackgaard would have no compunction against personally using physical violence in the pursuit of his goals. Maxwell had to follow through; he had no choice.

Then a different thought struck him: If his goal was now to prevent Blackgaard from corrupting Connie, then what he was about to do would fulfill that goal and satisfy Blackgaard, wouldn't it?

And just like that, the nefarious scheme he had planned became ennobled in his mind. He smiled broadly, pleased at his ingenuity. He'd need even more cleverness to complete the rest of what Blackgaard had tasked him to do without anyone getting hurt, but he knew he could ennoble that somehow as well. He was back in control.

The bell above the front door of Whit's End tinkled as the door swung open, and the person he was waiting for entered.

Lucy.

CHAPTER ELEVEN

Maxwell pressed himself back into the booth and watched Lucy hang her hat and coat on the rack by the door. Though they had met formally only yesterday, he remembered her from her frequent visits to the Odyssey Retirement Home with her church youth group. He wondered if she knew Rachael. *Probably not,* he thought. *She seems even more the conscientious type than Donna Barclay.*

After the tense exchange between Lucy and Connie

yesterday, though, he thought there might be something there he could use. Lucy's unmistakable attraction to him would also come in handy. And after Blackgaard's outburst, he knew he'd have to use both.

She walked into the main room and looked around, her back to the booth. *Let's have a little fun*, he thought. He cupped his hands over his mouth and said aloud in an otherworldly voice, "Luuucyyyy . . ."

She stopped, startled, her eyes darting around the room. "H-hello?" she said.

"Luuuucyyyy!"

She stiffened, and her voice trembled slightly. "W-who is that?"

He chuckled and said in his normal voice, "Just me—over here in the booth behind you."

Lucy wheeled around and then exhaled and smiled. "Oh, Richard! You scared me!"

"Aw, I'm sorry!" he said. "C'mon over and sit."

She crossed to the booth. "What are you doing here?"

He grinned. "Looking for you."

Her face flushed, and she sank into the bench oppo-site him. "Why?"

"Why? 'Cause I like you!"

Her face grew redder, and she frowned. "I don't see how you can like me after the way I acted last time you were here."

He furrowed his brow, pretending to remember. "You mean that little scene with Connie?"

"Yeah . . ." She looked at the table.

First, the setup. "Oh, that wasn't so bad. From what I could tell, you had good reason to be upset. You were trying to help somebody, and you got in trouble for it."

Lucy sighed and nodded. "Yeah, that seems to hap-pen a lot to me. But Connie was only trying to do her job too. And she was upset about getting fired from here. I shouldn't have gotten mad at her. That's why I came in. I want to find out where Connie lives so I can apologize to her."

Now the bait. "Lucy . . . how'd you like to do some-thing better for Connie than just apologize?"

Her face brightened. "I'd like it! But . . . what?"

Maxwell was about to respond when, out of the corner of his eye, he saw Eugene Meltsner emerge from the kitchen carrying a large bin of ice cream under each arm. Meltsner set them on the counter, opened the freezers under the countertop, and ducked into them, rearranging their contents so the new bins would fit.

Maxwell figured that was their cue to leave. "We can't talk in here," he said, scooting out of the booth. "Let's go outside and I'll tell you all about it. Okay?" He held out his hand for her.

Lucy looked unsure, then said, "Well . . . okay . . ." and placed her hand in his. He helped her to her feet, and they headed for the front door. As she put on her coat and hat, he glanced back at the counter. Meltsner's head and upper torso were still buried in the freezers.

Once outside, they took a walk around McAlister Park, and he told her his plan. *Next, the sell.* "So that's it, Lucy," he said with a small shrug. "What do you think?"

They stopped in front of a park bench. She looked torn. "I-I don't know, Richard."

"What's the matter?"

She sat. "I just don't know if I should do it."

He eased down beside her. "Why not?"

"'Cause . . . I'd be lying."

Ease her in . . . "No, you wouldn't, not really."

"'Not really'?" she said skeptically. "A lie is a lie, Richard."

Careful. "I know—you're right. But we're only doing it to make things better here, aren't we? I mean, that *is* what we want to do, isn't it, make things better?"

She looked confused. "Y-yes . . ."

Move in. "Look, do you think Connie wants to work at Whit's End again?"

"Yeah . . ."

"And do you think Mr. Whittaker wants her to work there again?"

"Yeah . . ."

"Well, the only way that's gonna happen is if they get together and talk about it, right?"

She leaned back. "Well . . . yeah . . ."

He held out his hands. "See? You're just helpin' them do what they already want to do! That's not lying!"

Her brow furrowed again. "It still doesn't seem right."

"What's not right? You'll be helping Connie, you'll be helping Mr. Whittaker, and you know what else?"

She looked at him. "What?"

Time for the net. "You'll be helping *me*, too." He took her hand. "I'd really appreciate it." He gave her his most charming smile. "Whaddya say?" He squeezed her hand gently, and her breath quickened as her face flushed completely.

She looked off but didn't pull her hand away. *C'mon . . . c'mon . . .* She took a deep breath and said hesitantly, "Tell me what I have to do again?"

Yes!

He felt the familiar rush of excitement—the conquest, the play, slowly reeling in the mark until finally . . . the score! There was no better feeling, just as Brownlow had taught him—

He stopped. A lump suddenly appeared in his throat, and a pang of guilt stabbed his conscience. He froze for a moment, then shook it off. *No. No! This is different!* Yes, he was using Lucy, but this time he was using someone for good—to protect Connie. *Yes, that's it!* And he would protect Lucy, too. He could handle this. *I'm still in control.*

"Richard?"

Her large brown eyes gazed at him with concern through her round glasses. He smiled again and responded smoothly, "I knew I could count on you! You're the best! All you have to do is go to Whit's End tomorrow morning at about a quarter past ten and make a phone call."

CHAPTER TWELVE

At precisely 10:15 the next morning, the phone rang at Connie's house. June answered it with a pleasant, "Kendall residence."

Through the receiver, she heard Lucy's filtered voice say, "Hi, is Connie there?"

"No, she went to the store. I'm expecting her back any minute, though. Can I take a message?"

Lucy cleared her throat. "Um, yeah, uh, this is Lucy, one of the kids at Whit's End."

"Oh, yes! I remember you!"

"Uh, yeah, well, could you tell Connie that Mr. Whittaker wants to talk to her, and that he wants her to meet him on Stone Bridge as soon as she can get there?"

June smiled. "Really? That's wonderful! She'll be very glad to hear it!"

"Yeah, I know," Lucy responded. She cleared her throat again.

"Are you feeling all right, Lucy dear?"

"Yeah, I-I'm fine," she stuttered, then added quickly, "Well, if you could give Connie the message, I'd really appreciate it. Bye, Mrs. Kendall."

"Okay, thank you, Lu—" Click. The line went dead. "—cy . . . um . . . bye." She hung up the receiver, frowned, and muttered, "Strange."

The huge barn doors groaned as they opened, and two loud whinnies greeted Tom Riley as he entered.

He smiled at the horses and said lovingly, "Well, good morning, Leah. Good morning, Miss Rachel! How are my two fine girls this morning?"

Leah and Rachel nickered.

Tom chuckled and continued. "Oh, that's good! I'll bet you're ready for breakfast, aren't you? Well, let's get you some nice, fresh hay, shall we?" He forked hay into both horses' troughs and then quickly mucked out their stalls as they munched on their breakfasts.

"Looks like you both could use new salt licks, too," Tom said. He retrieved the licks from the locker and began tying them to the stall gates. "You know, you girls are gonna have to amuse yourselves this morning."

The horses nickered again.

"Yeah, I know, but I have to go to town for a council meeting."

Leah snorted.

Tom chuckled again. "Well, I feel the same way, Leah, but I have to go 'cause we're takin' a vote." He finished tying off the licks. "There, all done. Now, I'll only be gone for a couple of hours, so you both just stay in the barn 'til I get back, okay?"

The horses whinnied a response, and he patted both on their necks.

"There's my good girls. Bye now!"

He turned and exited the barn, humming an old hymn, crossed the yard to his pickup, got in, started it up, and headed down his dirt driveway for the highway into town. He never looked in his rearview mirror, so he didn't see the shadowy figure emerge from the south orchard and race across the yard toward the barn.

Whit descended the stairs at Whit's End and saw Lucy on the phone. When she saw him, a look of alarm crossed her face, and he heard her mutter what sounded like a hasty "Bye"—though he couldn't make out to whom—and she quickly hung up.

"Lucy?" he said.

She swallowed hard, forced a smile, and said, "Oh, hi, Mr. Whittaker."

Whit also smiled. "You making a call or answering one?"

She glanced at the phone. "Oh, uh, making one. Mr. Whittaker, I have a note for you."

"A note?"

She fished it out of her coat pocket. "Yeah, uh, Connie came over to my house last night and asked me to give it to you this morning." She held out a folded piece of typewriter paper to him.

His brow furrowed. "Connie?"

"Yeah . . . I guess she didn't want to give it to you herself."

He took the note and opened it. It was typed. Odd. He read it aloud: "Whit: We have to talk. Please meet me at Stone Bridge at 10:30 a.m. Connie." He flipped over the paper, but the back was blank. "Stone Bridge? That's on the way out to Tom's house . . ." He glanced at the grandfather clock by the front door. "And it's past 10:15 now."

Lucy shrugged nervously. "I'm sorry, Mr. Whittaker, I got here as soon as I could."

He patted her shoulder. "I know you did, Lucy. It's just that I'm supposed to go to the town council meeting at 10:30." He contemplated the note again. "Hmm . . . I told Tom I'd be there, too." He rubbed his chin and took a deep breath. "Well, Connie is definitely more important." He refolded the note and pocketed it. "Listen, will you tell Eugene where I've gone, and that I'll be back later?"

Lucy nodded. "Sure." She looked at him intensely. "Mr. Whittaker, are you gonna hire Connie back?"

He smiled. "That's what I'm gonna find out at Stone Bridge, Lucy." He grabbed his coat and opened the front door, dinging the bell. "Bye!" He closed the door behind him.

Lucy sighed deeply and muttered, "Bye."

"I'm home!" Connie announced. She closed the back door and set shopping bags on the kitchen counter. "Mom?"

June called out from the other room, "Connie?"

"Yeah, I got all the stuff you wanted, except that the store was out of regular milk, so I got this 2 percent instead. Is that all right?"

June rushed into the kitchen, smiling broadly. "Never mind the milk! Guess what's happened!"

Connie gave her mom a puzzled grin and opened the fridge. "What?"

"Whit wants to see you!"

Connie nearly dropped the milk. "He does?"

"Yes!" June said, nodding. "Someone at his shop called while you were gone. He wants to meet you at Stone Bridge right away!" It was her turn to look puzzled. "I wonder why he wants to meet you there?"

Connie fairly threw the milk carton onto the shelf in the fridge and shoved the door closed. "Who cares, as long as he wants to see me! Do I look all right?"

June chuckled. "You look just fine, sweetheart."

Connie shuffled around the kitchen table and opened and closed her hands. "Oh, Mom . . . I'm so nervous!"

June grabbed her shoulders. "I'm sure everything will turn out fine. Take a breath."

Connie followed her mother's instructions—a deep inhale and slow exhale. She looked at her mom and then threw her arms around her neck. "Thanks, Mom." She released the hug and bolted for the door. "I'll let you know what happens!"

June brushed away a happy tear and called after her. "Bye, sweetheart!"

"Bye!"

Odyssey Town Hall was filled with the usual buzz of low conversations that preceded every town council meeting. Council members and the few citizens who attended such proceedings milled about, exchanging pleasantries and local gossip. Off to one side, Dr. Regis Blackgaard and Philip Glossman discussed the most pressing matter before the council that day.

Glossman dabbed the sweat from his upper lip

with a handkerchief. "The way I see it," he whispered harshly, "we still don't have enough votes to win. Of the five council members, I'm solidly behind you, and Riley is solidly against you. The other three sway according to popular opinion. I hope you brought more documentation about your plans for Blackgaard's Castle."

Blackgaard looked relaxed, as if he were on a stroll in the park. "I don't think we're going to be needing it, Philip," he intoned quietly. "Today, popular opinion will be on your side. Why don't you start the meeting?"

Glossman's eyes darted around the room. "But Riley isn't here," he said.

"No, he isn't." Blackgaard sniffed his boutonniere casually.

Glossman mopped his forehead and licked his lips. "Dr. Blackgaard—"

"You worry too much, Philip," Blackgaard interrupted, adjusting his shirt cuffs. "Just do your part and let me handle the rest."

Richard Maxwell peered out from the cover of the orchard and watched Tom Riley's truck rumble down his long dirt driveway and head out on the road running through the farm. Once the truck was obscured by the dust of the road, he emerged from the trees and slunk to the back side of the barn, carrying a container of kerosene.

He knew Blackgaard wanted him to set the barn afire, but he also knew he didn't have to go that far. Instead, he quickly gathered a pile of hay and deadwood from the trees, sloshed the kerosene all over it, and pulled a box of matches from his pocket. *Control,* he thought. The point was to keep Riley from the vote. A pile of burning debris that made it look as if the barn was burning would do the trick.

Maxwell peered around the barn and saw the dust from behind Riley's truck. *Good, not too far away.* He removed a match from the box, struck it, studied the small flame for a moment, then bent down and flicked it onto the pile.

The kerosene erupted into a small fireball. Maxwell yelped and jumped back instinctively, landing on his back. The flames grew, and the black smoke from the debris rose into the air. Suddenly, he realized his left arm was very hot. He looked over at it.

His shirt was on fire.

He had sloshed kerosene on it, and the fireball had ignited it. He jumped up with a roar and tore off the shirt, sending buttons flying everywhere. He tossed it to the side and scrambled away.

The shirt landed on a hay bale leaning against the barn wall. Maxwell turned back just in time to see it burst into flames, which seemed to leap up the wooden barn wall at an alarming rate. He watched it with frightened fascination, broken only by what sounded like screams coming from inside the barn. He froze in horror.

The horses!

Tom Riley continued humming the hymn happily as he drove, even managing to grind the old truck's gears in time with the tune. After one particularly loud grind, he glanced in his rearview mirror. What he saw there made him stop both the truck and his humming.

"What in the world!" he said aloud. "Smoke!" He rolled down his window and popped out his head. "Looks like it's comin' from—" An icy shiver shot up his spine, and his eyes widened with panic. "No!"

He slammed the truck into gear, and its steering column squealed in protest as he turned around and raced back to his farm and the column of black smoke that now billowed from it into the sky.

CHAPTER THIRTEEN

Stone Bridge was one of the lovelier spots on the outskirts of Odyssey. True to its name, it was a small bridge made of stone that spanned Trickle Creek, which was fed by Trickle Lake on Forest Mountain, and ran through several meadows, pine groves, and Tom Riley's farm. The bridge was set in one of the groves and was a popular spot for strolls, picnics, and lovers to go courting.

It was deserted this morning, however, Connie

noticed as she rode up to it on her bike. She saw no one except for the familiar figure of her former boss, John Avery Whittaker, who stood at the apex of the bridge span. Connie parked her bike at one side of the bridge, took a deep breath to stop her stomach from bouncing around her insides, and headed up the bridge to him. He turned to meet her. "Hi, Whit," she said.

"Hello, Connie," he replied.

"Sorry I'm late—" She stopped and rolled her eyes. "Why is that always the first thing I say to you?"

Whit smiled. "That's okay. I just got here myself."

There was an awkward pause. Whit gazed at her steadily, hopefully, with his piercing eyes. She finally took a deep breath. "Whit . . . I owe you an apology for the way I acted the last time I saw you. I really wanted to talk to you, but I guess I got kinda weirded out when I saw you'd hired Eugene back."

"Connie, there's a whole story behind that—"

She stopped him. "I know, I do. That's what Eugene said, and that's what I keep telling myself. But all these thoughts kept creeping into my head . . ." She lowered her eyes. "About you playing favorites . . . about you liking Eugene better than me . . ."

His gaze softened. "Oh, Connie. Listen, I owe you an apology too. I was pretty—how did you say it?—'weirded out' when I saw you with Richard Maxwell, so I didn't say the things I could have said, either."

Connie's brow furrowed. "But I'd only met him a couple of minutes before you came in. Besides, what's wrong with Richard?"

Whit shook his head. "It's a long story."

"Oh!" She brightened. "Well, it doesn't matter now. When I got your message, I knew everything was gonna be all right!"

He gave her a puzzled smile. "My message?"

"Yeah!" she said with a nod. "When my mom told me you called this morning, I was so excited I nearly jumped out of my skin!"

His puzzled look morphed into outright confusion. "Connie, I didn't call you."

She blinked. "You didn't?"

"No. I came here because of this note you sent to

me." He pulled it from his coat pocket and handed it to her.

She took it and said, "Note?" She opened it and scanned the words.

Whit nodded. "Lucy said you told her to give it to me . . ." His head jerked up with an epiphany. "And that was right after she hung up the phone. Oh, dear."

Connie also looked stunned. "Come to think of it, my mom didn't say *who* called this morning. She just said the *shop* called."

Whit chuckled. "Looks like Lucy engineered this whole thing."

Connie looked over the note, still perplexed. "But why?"

Whit shrugged. "Maybe so we could talk. Pretty nice of her."

Connie sighed heavily. "I don't know why she'd want to do anything nice for me, especially after what happened up at camp."

"Oh? What happened?"

Connie turned and looked at the creek. "Lucy and

another girl were caught outside their cabins after hours, and I had to send them home. I didn't want to. I even gave them both a second chance the first time they did it." She glanced at him. "But if I learned anything from getting fired, it's that there's a reason for rules, and when you break them, you have to suffer the consequences."

Whit's face broke into sheer delight. "*Really?*"

"Yeah, I realized that—" She glanced at him again and saw him beaming at her. "What? What did I say? Why are you smiling?"

"Connie, I hired Eugene back because I saw, first-hand, that he understood why I fired him. You've just shown me you understand too!"

"Oh!" she said, scarcely breathing. She swallowed. "So . . . where do we go from here?"

Whit smiled so wide that his face almost couldn't contain it. "Well," he said, bobbing up and down on the balls of his feet, "if you're not too busy—if you don't have any plans—I know of an ice cream, invention, and discovery emporium that . . . that . . ." He placed his hand on her arm tenderly. "That sure would love to have you come home."

Connie choked back tears. "Oh, Whit!" She grabbed his neck and hugged him as tightly as she could. He hugged her right back. It was a moment of pure bliss.

Suddenly they broke apart. "Do you smell . . . smoke?" he asked.

She nodded. "Yeah . . . " And then she saw it. She pointed behind him. "Look!"

Whit whipped around. "Good grief!" In the distance, a huge plume of black smoke billowed into the atmosphere.

"Somebody must be having one huge barbeque!" she marveled.

"That's no barbeque. Something's on fire! Something near Tom's place!" He took off toward his car.

Connie raced after him. "Hey! Wait for me!" she shouted.

They hopped in, Whit started the engine, and they peeled out, headed for Tom's farm.

A few minutes later, Philip Glossman gaveled the meeting to order. The room quieted. "Well, ladies and gentlemen," he began, "it appears that Mr. Riley had more important things to do than attend our town council meeting today. Perhaps he'll show up later, but in the meantime, I suggest we get on with the business at hand. And the first item on the agenda is the vote to grant a business license to Dr. Regis Blackgaard."

Maxwell sped around the barn and raced through its open front doors. The horses' eyes were wide with panic. Tongues of flame were now probing through the slats in the back wall and licking the interior. Smoke collected in the barn loft and was slowly descending to fill the structure. He spied the horses' nameplates attached to their stall gates: Leah . . . and Rachel. His sister's image flashed through his mind—*Rachael!*

He bolted to the horses' stalls to open them, but the animals' fear of the flames, the smoke, and the stranger in their midst made them buck, rear, and kick about their pens, stomping at their stall gates, nipping at him with their teeth, and lashing out with their forehooves. He fell back, momentarily more afraid of them than he was of the fire, looked around the barn, and decided on a different tack.

He grabbed a bucket and ran out into the yard, looking for a water source, and quickly found one— a pump and trough next to a round pen near the back of the barn. He raced to it, shoved the bucket under the faucet, and turned on the spigot. Water cascaded into the bucket.

As he filled the pail at the back of the barn, Tom Riley drove up to the front of it. He slammed on his brakes, leaped out of the truck, bolted to the barn, and grabbed the fire extinguisher sitting just inside the door. Maxwell, in his panic, had failed to notice it.

Riley cooed soothing words to Leah and Rachel, popped the pin on the extinguisher handle, and was just about to spray down the back wall when the tiny flames creeping up it flashed into an inferno.

Maxwell had filled the bucket to the top. When he lifted it, he realized it was so heavy that if he tried to run to the front of the barn with it, half the water would slosh out before he got there. So he decided to go to the fire's source on the back wall. He lugged the bucket in that direction and saw a sight that made his heart nearly stop.

The fire had not only crept up the barn wall, but it had also gone back toward the pile of debris and had surrounded and lit the container of kerosene. Without thinking, Maxwell lifted the water bucket and, with a loud groan, heaved its entire contents onto the container.

The fire exploded. Billows of flame and jets of burning kerosene spat in all directions, but mainly at the barn's rear wall. Maxwell was knocked on his back again. Hissing, scalding steam mixed with the smoke to block his vision and singe his hair and eyebrows.

In the barn, Riley was also knocked backward. His

head slammed against the barn door, and he thudded to the ground in the doorway, unconscious. Leah and Rachel screamed, bucked, and reared in terror.

Maxwell struggled to his feet, shielded his face from the flames, and trudged through the smoke to the front of the barn. He saw Riley lying in the doorway, not moving. He took a step toward the old farmer, but he stopped when he heard an engine accelerate and saw through the smoke a car turn onto the farm's dirt road.

Someone is coming! You can't be seen! Get clear! He slunk backward out of sight of the car, then raced to his camouflaged spot in the grove of apple trees. *This is not how it was supposed to go! It wasn't supposed to happen this way!* He watched the car race up and stop behind Riley's truck, and Whittaker and Connie get out.

"Whit!" Connie screamed.

"Go in the house and call the fire department, quick!" Whittaker barked at her.

"All right!" She headed toward the house.

Whittaker called out, "Tom! Tom!"

Why don't they see Riley?

Then, just before Connie got to the house, she screamed and pointed. "Whit! He's lying in the doorway!"

They raced to him, pulled him away from the barn, and turned him over gently. "He's unconscious!" Whittaker said. "Help me with him!"

Connie trembled visibly, and her voice shook as she prayed, "Dear Jesus, please let him be okay!"

They sat him upright, and Whittaker smacked him smartly on the face a couple of times. Riley coughed and sputtered.

The horses screamed and pounded at their stalls.

"Whit . . ." Riley gasped, "the horses . . . get the horses!" He lapsed into a coughing fit.

Whittaker jerked him to his feet. "Take him over to the porch, Connie!" Whittaker ordered, and then he bolted back to the barn.

"Be careful, Whit!" she screamed after him, putting Riley's arm around her shoulders and leading him to the porch. She sat him on the steps and ran inside the house.

Whittaker disappeared inside the barn.

Several seconds that seemed like hours passed.

Maxwell barely breathed. The flames consumed more and more of the barn. Smoke billowed out the doors. *This wasn't supposed to happen!* Maxwell thought.

Suddenly he heard Whittaker yell, "Hyaahh! Hyaaah!" and almost instantly two horses burst out of and away from the flaming structure, followed closely by a coughing and spluttering Whittaker. Whittaker ran over to Riley on the porch. Connie exited the house with a pitcher of water and some cups and joined them. "The fire department's on its way!" she exclaimed.

Whittaker nodded and gasped. "Leah and Rachel are all right, Tom. They're out."

Maxwell felt so relieved, he nearly fainted. *Everyone's okay. At least everyone is okay.*

Connie yelled, "And just in time, Whit! The roof's coming down!"

The barn collapsed in on itself, crashing down to the earth in a cloud of dust, smoke, and flame. Maxwell, who could finally feel his legs again, used that distraction to beat a hasty and unnoticed retreat back through the orchard.

At the porch, Connie poured water from the pitcher into the cups and handed one to each man. Whit grasped Tom's shoulder. "Are you okay?" he asked.

Tom gulped his water and coughed. "Yeah. I'm all right."

"What happened?" Connie asked.

Tom wet his handkerchief with water from his cup and wiped the dust and ash from his eyes and face. "I . . . was on my way to the council meeting . . . I looked in my rearview mirror and saw smoke . . . so I came back to this! . . . I tried to get the horses . . . but the flames flared up, and I got knocked silly."

Connie poured him more water. "I wonder how it happened?" she asked.

"I must've . . . left something flammable . . . lying out," Tom gasped.

Whit looked back at the still-blazing structure. "Or someone set the fire deliberately," he said.

The front wall and doorframe now collapsed to the ground. Tom watched in anguish. "But why would anybody want to set my barn on fire, Whit?" Tears streamed down his cheeks. "Why?"

Back in town, Glossman presided over the vote. "Mr. Finster?" he intoned.

"Aye."

"Mr. Hirnsby?"

"Aye."

"Mr. Donohue?"

"Aye."

"And I also vote aye. That's four aye votes, with one default." Glossman smiled. "Congratulations, Dr. Blackgaard. You have your license."

The assemblage applauded politely as Blackgaard rose and bowed genially toward the council. "Thank you, Mr. Glossman, and you other council members," he said. "I'm sure this is just the beginning of a long and profitable association between myself, Blackgaard's Castle, and the town of Odyssey."

Eugene, Connie, and Whit sat quietly in the waiting area of Odyssey General Hospital. It had been just Connie and Eugene for the longest time, but finally Whit emerged from a treatment room with his arm wrapped in a bandage and his hair looking a bit frizzy. He assured his employees that he was all right, then joined them as they continued to sit in silent vigil, each lost in thought.

Finally, Connie stretched and sighed. "I wish

someone would tell us something!" she said. "How long have we been here, anyway?"

Eugene checked his watch. "Three hours, 57 minutes, 13 seconds," he said quietly.

Connie squeezed Whit's hand. "How's your arm?" she asked.

"Fine, Connie. Just a little sore."

There was another long silence. They watched as several patients were wheeled in and out of rooms on gurneys. Connie took another deep breath and stood up. "*Boy* do I wish someone would tell us something!" She surveyed the room. "Does anyone want anything from the cafeteria, a cup of coffee or—"

"Whit?" a voice said.

They all turned. Doctor Farber was headed for them. Whit and Eugene rose from their chairs as she approached. "Hello, Dr. Farber," Whit said.

Farber spied the bandage. "How's the arm?"

"A little singed," Whit answered with a shrug. "I've had much worse."

The doctor smiled. "I understand you've been waiting to hear about the Cunningham-Schultz girl?"

"Yes, we all have."

Farber consulted her chart. "Well, she's pretty banged up. A possible concussion and some nasty bruises. We're going to have to watch her closely. She's had quite a shock—literally."

"I know the feeling," Whit replied. "But . . . she'll be all right?"

The doctor nodded. "I think it's safe to say so, yes."

Connie heaved a sigh of relief and leaned against Eugene. "Oh, thank the Lord!"

Eugene pushed her back upright.

"Can we see her?" asked Whit.

"Not right now," Farber demurred. "I gave her a sedative in emergency. She needs all the rest she can get. Her parents are watching her, and I'd like to keep it that way for a while."

"We understand," Whit said. "Thank you."

Farber took a breath. "That wasn't the only reason I

came to talk with you. I also brought *you* a visitor." She turned back and called, "Uh, Sheriff?"

Eugene gulped. "Sheriff?"

"If you'll excuse me, I have other patients to attend to," Farber said.

"Of course. Thanks again, Doctor," Whit said.

Farber patted Whit on the shoulder and walked away as the sheriff approached.

The sheriff tipped his hat and said, "'Lo, Whit."

Whit nodded. "Bill."

The sheriff sighed. "I don't know how to say this, Whit, without comin' right out and sayin' it. We're gonna have to conduct an investigation into this incident."

"Investigation?" Connie squawked. "It was an accident!"

Whit held up a finger. "Connie . . ."

She backed off.

Whit turned back to the sheriff. "I understand, Bill."

"Well, you know what that means," the sheriff said

apologetically. "Now, it'll just be temporary, until the investigation is over." He pulled a paper from his back pocket. "I got a court order here . . ."

Both Connie and Eugene started at the sight of the order, but Whit continued before they could say anything. "Of course, Bill. I'll cooperate with you fully. But you won't need the court order. I was gonna close down Whit's End myself anyway."

This time, he couldn't stop his employees' outbursts.

"What?"

"Mr. Whittaker!"

Whit held up his hands, and that stopped them from going any further, at least temporarily.

The sheriff nodded. "All right, Whit. We'll work out the details in the morning." He tipped his hat again. "G'night, all." He turned and strolled away.

"Good night, Bill," Whit called after him.

Connie and Eugene were on him almost immediately:

"Close it down?"

"But why?"

Whit frowned. "I'm conducting an investigation of my own. I have to make sure Whit's End is safe."

"But it was an accident, Whit!" Connie implored. "An accident!"

Whit squeezed her hand and Eugene's arm. "I know, I know . . ." He looked them both in the eyes sincerely and with great affection, then dropped his gaze to the floor. "Look . . . my place was designed and built to *help* kids. And now it's done just the opposite. I have to make sure that doesn't happen again."

He dropped his holds on them, took a step back, and looked up at them again. "I'm sorry, but until further notice, Whit's End is closed."